OUTRAGEOUS OLIVIA

MAIL ORDER BRIDES RESCUE SERIES, BOOK #6

JO GRAFFORD, WRITING AS
JOVIE GRACE

ISBN: 978-1-63907-020-6

GET A FREE BOOK!

Join my mailing list to be the first to know about new releases, free books, special discount prices, Bonus Content, and giveaways.

https://BookHip.com/GNVABPD

ACKNOWLEDGMENTS

Many, many thanks to my beta readers and editor, Cathleen Weaver, for reading and sharing their thoughts on this story. I am also wildly grateful to my Cuppa Jo Readers on Facebook for reading and loving my books!

ABOUT THIS SERIES

The only mail order bride company with an insurance policy enforced by the Gallant Rescue Society — *No extra cost!*

The Gallant Rescue Society Oath

"I hereby solemnly pledge my gun and my honor to the Gallant Rescue Society.

To be called upon day or night.

To rescue any Bride-To-Be from any undesirable circumstance on her journey to meet her Groom.

To return her (if at all possible) with her virtue intact to the Boomtown Mail Order Brides Company.

No questions asked.

So help me, God."

CHAPTER 1: ANOTHER MISTAKE

OLIVIA

*O*livia Rothschild stood fuming beside the pianoforte in the grand parlor of her aunt's estate home in Boston. It was true she was forever landing herself in scrapes; but this time, it wasn't her fault. It truly was *not!* How could she have possibly known the debonair Alec Grenville wasn't an actual marquis? That he'd merely been posing as his cousin, Charles — the *real* marquis — because they looked enough alike to pass as twins?

Every hopeful mama with a daughter of marriageable age had their assessing eye on the marquis, including Olivia's guardian, the highly fashionable Beatrice Rothschild — a wealthy spinster who'd never risked the perils of marriage, herself. That was why Olivia was in a bucketful of trouble right now. If only her nosy rival, Diana Edgerton, hadn't witnessed Olivia kissing Alec during their carriage ride this afternoon! La, but the chit had been quick to spread the poisonous tale, and now Olivia's reputation was extremely compromised.

Her aunt made her stew a full hour before sailing into the room in one of her newest gowns, a mouth-watering creation of pure midnight blue silk imported from the Orient. Her Mandarin collar was edged in delicately tooled ivory lace, and tiny pheasants flitted across her bodice in silver and gold threads.

"Well?" she demanded without preamble. "What do you have to say for yourself this time, niece?"

Olivia spread her hands. Though she'd had plenty of time to think about what she was going to say, she'd managed to come up with exactly nothing that would pacify her aunt. "Aunt Bee," she entreated softly. It was her pet name for her aunt, a nickname that normally made her melt a few degrees.

Beatrice Rothschild's fair, classical features hardened. "This is not the time for sweet nothings and apology kisses, child. We've a real problem on our hands!"

"I am aware," she mumbled miserably, looking down at her hands. She twisted them tightly together. "You said you wanted me to engage the marquis's attentions. I honestly believed I was doing what you asked when I—"

"You kissed the wrong man!" her aunt hissed. "I specifically instructed you to flirt with the marquis and the marquis only. I cannot believe you botched it so horribly." She produced a fan and waved it in agitation at her face. "When a young woman sets out to be indiscreet, she must do it with more care. Most unfortunately, you've given Diana every reason to flap her tongue at your expense. It'll be a miracle if your reputation isn't in shreds by morning."

Olivia dragged in a tortured breath and asked the question that had been plaguing her most of the afternoon. "Does this mean you will force me to marry Alec?"

Her aunt's aristocratic brows rose, wrinkling her high forehead. "Force is a strong word, my dear. I prefer to think of it as self preservation. Alec may not have the title we hoped to secure for you, but he is still a Grenville. That is a name that will open many doors in society for you."

For us, you mean. Olivia had heard the speech a thousand times about how to elevate one's standing in the world through a proper marriage to a man bearing the right surname. She didn't care a fig about such things, but they mattered to her aunt. Greatly! If the woman was anything, she was a social climber. She was also a skilled manipulator of men. If she decided Olivia needed to marry the man she'd kissed, the deed was as good as done.

"So you *do* mean for me to marry him." Olivia bit her lower lip.

"Do you have a better scheme to save your heavily besmirched reputation, niece?"

Scheme! This couldn't be happening! One honest mistake and her aunt wanted to turn her entire future into one of her diabolical *schemes*? Olivia raised and lowered her shoulders. "I could leave town for a few months. Claim an urgent matter of business in New York or the like." Most of her late father's warehouses were located along the Hudson River. It wouldn't be that much of a stretch to claim she needed to pay a visit to his business holdings.

Her aunt shuddered. "And remind everyone in Boston that all your money was acquired in trade? No, thank you! It would be social suicide for both of us."

For you. I do not care one whit. I never have. Olivia couldn't believe her aunt was seriously considering making her marry over one small indiscretion — an indiscretion the woman helped to create with her own less-than-savory courting advice. "How soon do I have to decide, Aunt Bee?"

Her aunt snapped her fan closed and tapped it against her palm. "Immediately."

"Tonight?" Olivia's brain felt close to exploding. Everything was happening too fast.

"Yes! We have to get ahead of the rumors before they spiral out of control and ruin us."

Us. At least her aunt was finally admitting the real reason for her paranoia. She wanted to continue to be one of the belles of high society in Boston. She wanted to hold her head high and have the doors to all the exclusive dress makers, dining establishments, and clubs remain open to her. One black spot on a woman's reputation, and all those doors could slam shut...permanently.

Olivia reached for her wide-brimmed walking hat and her reticule. "I need some fresh air," she murmured, feeling lightheaded.

Her aunt's frown deepened. "Where are you going? I thought I made it clear we need to act now. You and I should jointly call on the Grenvilles this very evening. Fortunately for you, I am a dear friend of their grandfather. He will hear me out and listen to reason. I am certain of it!"

Olivia pushed open the front door, feeling like she was about to suffocate. "I'll return within the hour and give you my decision then." After she had the chance to clear her head...

"Within the hour! So help me, Olivia! If you walk out of here while I am—"

Unable to listen to another word without screaming, Olivia firmly shut the door behind her. A faint autumn breeze enveloped her and propelled her down the quiet, ritzy avenue towards the much busier business section of the city. Feeling like a boat without an anchor, she drifted aimlessly past shop windows, hardly knowing where she was heading. Her black lace-up boots felt like they were full of lead. Her heart was equally heavy.

It had been five full years since her mother had passed and three since her father had departed. Nothing had been the same since. Her Aunt Bee had tried to step in and serve as both her father and mother, but her aunt's social climbing aspirations had brought little but misery to their household.

Even the servants stepped lightly around her and avoided direct encounters as much as possible.

Oh, how Olivia wished her parents could have lived long enough to raise her themselves! No doubt they'd possessed a fault or two, but she couldn't remember a single one of their onerous traits. All she could recall was how kind they were to everyone and how loved they were by everyone. They'd also been patient and long-suffering with their spirited only daughter, forever encouraging her to be kind and good.

"I'm not the young woman they would have raised me to be." She muttered the words aloud to punish her own ears. Under her aunt's tutelage, she was fast becoming a person she wasn't proud to look at in the mirror.

She paused in front of a shop window on 14th Street and Broad. It was bathed in the glow of the setting sun. Her own reflection scowled back — a stylish debutante of nineteen years (nearly twenty) with long blonde hair twisted in an elegant up-do. Her gown was tailored uniquely for her by Boston's most sought-after seamstress, Yvonne Taylor. Only the deepest pockets could afford the woman's exclusive designs.

Olivia's cream wool coat with its fur cuffs was unbuttoned. The gown she wore beneath it boasted a bodice of hand-crocheted lace, with a deep berry silk overlay and a berry and white pinstriped underskirt. Her bustle consisted of ruched gold silk that cascaded past her ankles to a short train. Normally, the sight of so much finery would have made her feel like a princess. This evening, it merely filled her with guilt and regret.

I am vain and selfish, spoiled and over-indulged. That is why I am continually landing myself in deplorable situations. Living from party to party the past few years certainly hadn't given her any resounding sense of accomplishment. Nor had it provided much in the way of personal happiness...

Quite the opposite. Her busy socialite calendar had worn her down, body and soul. Somehow along the way, Diana Edgerton, who'd been her best friend as a child, had become her biggest rival. They were one hair's breadth short of declaring themselves enemies.

Regrettably, Olivia also no longer viewed any of the young men of her acquaintance on their merit, but rather on the size of their bank accounts and their ability to advance her place in society. She had no one left she counted as a true friend. She supposed she had her aunt to thank for that. It was a dismal thought.

And now she was being backed into a corner, forced to consider marrying a man she didn't love.

Alec Grenville. Though she'd shamelessly flirted with him and carelessly kissed him, she'd felt nothing afterwards. No sweet or tender feelings. No sense of attachment. No stirring of emotions, whatsoever.

I don't want to continue down this path. A stab of self-pity shook Olivia. It was followed by a mouthful of bitter remorse and the dreaded certainty that she must do something drastic to change her course. Otherwise, she would be lost forever.

I no longer wish to be a person who goes through the motions of life without wholly engaging my heart, intellect, and energy. I want to live — truly live. I want to love and be loved. And when it came time for her to marry, she wanted the kind of marriage her parents had enjoyed — one full of affection, laughter, and joy.

"I don't want this," she choked in a voice that was barely audible. "I'd rather die." *I don't want the future Aunt Bee has chosen for me.*

A man lightly cleared his throat, jolting her from her distress.

"May I help you, madame?"

Help me?

Her gaze fastened on the reflection of the man standing beside her in the picture window. *Nobody can help me out of the kind of trouble I'm in, certainly not a perfect stranger.*

He possessed a rangy build and was taller than her — quite a bit taller, in fact. Most people were. At five feet two, she was a good six or eight inches shorter than him, even in the elevated heels of her walking boots. The passers-by in the busy street moved in a distorted blur behind their heads.

She swiveled away from his reflection to face the man himself and stopped short. He wasn't the handsomest man she'd ever met, but he was by far the most striking. She couldn't quite put her finger on the reason.

Why did you stop on this particular street to address me, of all people? "A good evening to you, sir." She nodded at him in what she hoped was a polite but dismissive manner. However, she couldn't help casting a quick, admiring glance at his suit. He wore a well tailored black blazer over silk black trousers, and her critical eye told her his top hat rested on a fresh haircut. Against her will, her gaze finished sliding across his features and found his dark one assessing her with genuine concern.

He offered her a polite, half-apologetic smile she found more intriguing than ever. *Have we met? Do I know you?* In seconds, her overwrought mind ran over dozens of fashionable young men's faces in her memories and came up empty.

He bent his tall frame to peer more closely at her. "Pardon me if I seem overly forward, but you appear distressed. If there is anything I can do to help...?" His voice was a soothing baritone, perfectly modulated to inspire trust. "A cup of hot tea perhaps, if you step inside my office?"

"Your office?"

"Yes. I'm Jordan Branson. You might have heard of me." He held out a gloved hand, which she pretended not to see.

No, I've never heard of you. We clearly do not move in the same circles. In no hurry to share her own name, she narrowed her gaze on the building in question. Her lips parted in surprise at the sign in gilded letters surrounded by wildflowers. She'd not noticed it before.

Boomtown Mail Order Brides

She took a stumbling step back. "You run a bridal agency?" *Egad!* If she had any sense left in her, she would take off running and never look back.

His hand shot out to steady her elbow. "Are you well?" he asked quickly.

She yanked her arm away, as if his touch stung. "Mr. Branson, if you must know, I am already being pressured to consider a marriage I do not want. Your services are truly the last thing I need this evening." She shuddered, hating how rude she sounded but meaning every word of her outburst.

To her surprise, he looked even more concerned. "Just Jordan, please. No need to call me Mister." He reached around her to open the door to his office, which she suddenly realized she'd been half-blocking all this time. No wonder he'd accosted her. She was impeding his progress. She took another step back, feeling foolish.

"Please come in," he urged gently. "For tea and nothing else. I'll not badger you with any sales pitches. I promise."

As if she wasn't already in enough trouble! Hobnobbing with another dashing stranger certainly wasn't going to solve anything, yet Olivia found her feet following him inside. The temperature in the air warmed several degrees, thanks to a fire leaping in a whitewashed brick hearth.

She studied the room in surprise. It wasn't at all what she'd expected. There were no harem-esque red rugs or dark velvet curtains. Instead, the area was open and spacious, light and inviting. White eyelet lace curtains framed the windows, and a set of blue and white striped chairs were arranged to form a cozy sitting area.

"It's a lovely office." Her cultured tastes could find no fault.

"Thank you. If you'd like, I'll hang up your coat." He waited patiently while she hesitated, then shrugged out of it and handed it over. "Please, have a seat and allow me to serve that tea I mentioned."

She selected one of the striped chairs and gingerly sat while he removed his hat and hung it on a hook against the wall. In moments, he made his way back to the sitting area with two steaming teacups in hand.

"Thank you." She reached for it, all the while wondering why she'd accepted his invitation to step inside the building. A bridal agency, of all outlandish places! *Mercy! My brain is sorely addled this evening.*

"My pleasure." He took a seat across from her and sipped on his tea. Though he continued to watch her over the top of his teacup, there was nothing censuring in his gaze, which could only mean one thing. He hadn't yet recognized her. As promised, he didn't launch into any sales pitches about becoming a mail-order bride. In fact, he didn't speak at all. They sat in companionable silence for several, much-needed minutes of calm.

Eventually, curiosity got the better of her. "Why?" she demanded, lowering her teacup. "Why do you do this?" She gave a humorless laugh. "Most men of my acquaintance spend endless amounts of energy dodging commitments, whereas you… specialize in them?"

"I do." He smiled, and the worry lines cleared from his forehead. "It's not the shortest story. I doubt you have the time for it."

She didn't, but she caught her breath at his smile. Dear, heavens! The man had a lethal smile. Most women she knew would have swooned beneath its charm.

He set down his teacup on a side table and leaned in her

direction, resting his elbows on his knees. "The short version is, I've been running this business with my brother, Colt, ever since our sister, MaryAnne, disappeared out west."

"Disappeared!" Olivia, who'd raised her cup for another sip, left her teacup suspended in mid-air.

"She signed a mail-order bride contract with a dubious firm before my brother and I could stop her, rode a train to Arizona, and we haven't seen her since." His voice turned rough. "It was a few years ago."

"I am sorry for your loss." Her own troubles suddenly seemed less acute.

His brown eyes turned flinty. "I am not ready to claim a loss, Miss, er..."

"Olivia Rothschild," she supplied, forgetting she'd intended to keep that detail to herself.

To his credit, Jordan Branson didn't flicker an eyelid at the sound of her name, though he surely must have recognized it. Her name, face, and exploits had been splashed across every gossip rag in the east at some point or another.

He nodded to acknowledge her tardy introduction, but continued his vent. "Neither is Colt. Until someone sends us a body to bury, we will continue to hope. And search," he added grimly. His jaw clenched as he settled back in his seat.

She nodded, approving of his determination and grit. *Now, that's true love! And a purpose worth fighting for!* One she might partake in, herself, if she chose to disappear for a few months instead of marrying against her will. The thoughts formed and took shape in her mind. Words bubbled forth next and came tumbling out. "Although I've no wish to sign any of your horrifying contracts, perhaps we could help each other."

His mouth twisted. "I appreciate your optimism, Miss Rothschild, but I highly doubt it." The raking gaze he cast over her person was clear. He knew who she was and didn't take her any more seriously than her aunt did.

Well, that was going to change! Olivia straightened her spine. She was tired of being dismissed as a useless debutante. She was tired of having her life planned out for her, as if she didn't possess the wherewithal intellect to make a single decision for herself. La, if she was being honest with herself, she was tired of Boston, itself!

She folded her hands in her lap and leaned forward. "As it turns out, I've decided to leave town for a few months, until the rumors surrounding my latest indiscretion die down." He could think what he wanted of that. She was done with pretenses. "There is no reason I cannot make a trip out west and use my extensive resources to help you look for your sister." She arched a brow at him, daring him to contradict her. Even he could not deny her access to wealth and contacts.

"Make a trip west?" Jordan Branson hooked a finger in his collar and tugged. "To search for a young woman you've never met?" He shook his head. His expression reflected a strange mixture of doubt and hope. "I reckon it's my turn to ask why."

She smiled and spread her hands, knowing she had his attention at last — his real and undivided attention. "I've no wish to continue living the life of a debutante. I want a project I can throw my heart and energy into." She briefly caught her lower lip between her teeth, hoping she didn't sound too naive to a man of his vast matchmaking experience. "I want to do something good for a change." *There.* She braced herself for the holes he would surely shoot in her idea.

All she received was a look of pure male fascination and another one of his slow, devastating smiles. "From what I've heard about you, Miss Rothschild, you might actually be up to the task."

Her heart flip-flopped in her chest at his smile, though a flush rose to her cheeks at his words. She knew he did not necessarily mean them as a compliment. "Please assure me you're not referring to a certain deplorable nickname of mine." She watched for his reaction through lowered lashes.

His smile widened, and he steepled his fingers. "Whatever do you mean, Outrageous Olivia?"

She groaned and averted her flaming face. "Yes. That one." On one hand, she was mortified. On the other hand, it was strangely liberating to hear her nickname spoken aloud without a sliver of judgment. The man seemed more amused than scandalized by her reputation.

She could have kissed him for his kind acceptance of who she was. *Wait, stop! No more kisses. No more even thinking about kisses.* A kiss was what had gotten her into this mess in the first place.

CHAPTER 2: A SYMPATHETIC EAR

JORDAN

ou would journey west to help me search for my sister, eh? Bridal candidates generally walked through Jordan's office door looking for *his* assistance, not the other way around. It was a preposterous suggestion, yet he found himself fighting an inner battle over it. The idea of enlisting the help of someone with such vast resources was tempting, and he wasn't merely referring to Miss Rothschild's financial resources. A woman of her social status could move in circles he couldn't move in and speak to people who might never confide in a man, much less a matchmaker. In the short time they'd conversed, he also deduced she was intelligent and witty. And if her reputation was any indication, she was incorrigible — someone not accustomed to taking no for an answer. A force to be reckoned with, according to the tabloids..

Alas, she didn't look a day older than MaryAnne the year she'd disappeared. He couldn't risk the wellbeing of another young woman, not even for such a worthy cause.

Truth be told, you have no idea what you are offering, lass. "Have you traveled much, Miss Rothschild?" he inquired in a mild tone, searching for the right words to turn down her gracious, albeit ill-advised, offer.

All too many young ladies sauntered into his office, thinking the notion of traveling west sounded romantic; and it was...or had the potential to be. However, a good number of them liked the idea more than the following-through part. He generally turned away more business than he accepted. Why just this morning, he'd sent a lovely young miss home after discovering she'd merely had a tiff with her affianced and wished to punish him by signing a mail-order bride contract.

She took her time responding, adopting a sad, faraway expression. "I've traveled very little since I lost my parents a few years back, Mr. Branson." She fiddled with the handle of her teacup.

"I am sorry to hear it," he said gently. "Did you travel much before?" Uncovering the background and motivations of a potential client was very important during the initial interview. Though Miss Rothschild claimed she wasn't interested in becoming one of his mail-order bridal candidates, his instincts told him otherwise. It wasn't unusual for a well-bred young woman to pretend to be mortified at the thought of meeting her future husband through the mail. The fact was, Miss Olivia Rothschild had visited his office for a reason, and it had taken very little urging for her to step inside. He would treat her like a client until she gave him any reason to view her differently.

"We traveled often," she confessed. "Father owned warehouses up and down the Hudson River."

Which now belonged to her, beneath the auspices of a man of business and a socialite guardian. Or so said the gossip rags...

Miss Rothschild's animated features softened dreamily.

"Plus, he liked to visit his overseas offices every year in Bristol and La Rochelle."

He sat up straighter in his chair. Perhaps the young woman sitting in front of him had seen more of the world than he'd originally presumed. "You've been to both England and France?" he asked carefully.

"I made the voyage six times." The dreaminess in her expressive blue eyes was replaced by a world weariness a body didn't often see in someone so young. "Father continued to take me with him, even after Mother passed." There was a catch in her voice. "That was when he started allowing me to accompany him on his inland trips, as well. He had to make special arrangements with the headmistress of my finishing school to travel with a private tutor, so I did not fall behind in my studies."

The sadness in her voice wrenched at his heartstrings. Because of MaryAnne, he understood what it felt like to lose a loved one. Unlike him, however, Miss Rothschild didn't possess the faint hope of a reunion someday, at least not this side of glory. She'd buried her parents. They weren't coming back. MaryAnne might not, either. Then again, he had hope.

He forced a smile he didn't feel. "And where did you venture inland, Miss Rothschild?" He knew it was foolish of him to keep their conversation going, but he found himself loathing the idea of bringing it to an end and sending her on her way. There was something poignantly arresting about Olivia Rothschild. The more she spoke, the more he sensed an underlying urgency to her voice, an agitated verve to her gestures, and a pink tinge to her cheeks that could no longer be explained by the brisk late-October breezes outdoors — not after sitting inside and sipping tea with him for this long. Though it was technically no business of his, he was unaccountably anxious to uncover the reason for her distress.

She set her teacup down on the ornately carved end table

beside her chair. "All the way to the east coast, Mr. Branson. Father was determined to teach me everything he could about shipping and trade. He introduced me to the owners and executives of his subsidiary firms. He showed me first-hand how commodities are shipped from farms and mines to the receiving factories, and how the finished goods are then shipped to wholesalers and shop owners across the country." Without warning, her voice grew shaky, and her blue eyes stretched enormously wide.

"Miss Rothschild! Is everything alright?" For the briefest of moments, he wondered if she'd caught sight of a spider or some other menace. All too quickly, he realized she was simply fighting to hold back tears. They formed a glassy sheen over her eyes and gathered like a storm. Then they broke free.

"No!" she gasped. "It is not." Her classically lovely features crumpled, and she clapped a hand over her eyes. With the other hand, she blindly fished in her reticule and unearthed a lacy white handkerchief.

He watched in amazement and dismay as the most outrageously incorrigible debutante in the city wept her heart out in the middle of his office. By George, he was Jordan Branson! Co-owner of the Boomtown Mail Order Brides Agency. He was accustomed to female vapors and tears. He was armed with hot tea, cozy furniture, and a sympathetic ear. But in all his days, he'd not witnessed such a moving display of emotion. The breathtakingly beautiful young heiress wept like she was losing her parents all over again, like her very soul was breaking.

"Miss Rothschild," he cried in a low voice, feeling helpless. It was impossible to even begin addressing her problem when he had no idea what it was. He pushed himself from his chair and took a knee in front of her. "Please tell me what I can do to help you. I can run fetch a doctor, if need be. A family member. Whoever or whatever you require."

"No, please," she sobbed into her handkerchief. "Th-that is the v-very last thing I wish for. I, er…" Her shoulders shook, and she dragged in several whimpering gulps of air as she sought to regain control of herself.

He gripped the arms of her chair, quite prepared to catch her if she swooned.

Thus, when she lowered her handkerchief and opened her eyes at last, their faces were only inches apart.

"Oh!" she gasped, jolting in her seat. "Mr. Branson!" She clamped her rosy lips together, and her already mottled cheeks flushed an even brighter pink.

He lowered his arms from her chair and straightened to give her more space, but he did not immediately rise. "As I stated before, madam, I am at your service. Whatever I can do to assist you." He waved a hand. "If it is within my power, I will make it happen."

She swallowed hard and nodded. "Very well. I need to leave town. Quickly, sir."

He frowned, unsurprised to hear it. "Are you in any danger?"

"Not physically, no." She dabbed at her eyes with her sodden handkerchief. "But I will be forced to marry someone I do not wish to marry if I remain in Boston." She drew a shuddery breath. "He is a heartless prankster. A rogue with no care for anything but the next fox hunt or the next hand of cards. I cannot marry him. I cannot!" she snapped with such venom that he blinked. "It would be better for me to sign one of your ridiculous contracts than to do so. At the very least, you would match me with a man who wishes to marry and settle down. Isn't that how it works, Mr. Branson?"

Though her general assessment of his matchmaking

services was correct, for the life of him he couldn't stomach the thought of pairing her off with the next would-be groom on his waiting list.

"I was under the impression you did not wish to marry," he said quickly.

"Oh, but I do!" Her long blonde lashes fluttered prettily against her cheeks, and she seemed unable to meet his gaze any longer. "More than anything. I miss having a family of my own. I miss…belonging to someone. If it is unladylike to mention such a thing, then so be it." Her chin came up, and her stormy blue eyes met his defiantly.

He snorted. "I am a matchmaker, Miss Rothschild. I happen to be in the business of dealing with matters of the heart."

"I am not seeking to be dealt with or handled, Mr. Branson," she snapped. "I was simply stating facts. Once you know what it is like to love and be loved, nothing else can fill the void when it is taken away from you." Her eyes grew damp again, making him fear another bout of weeping was forthcoming.

"I do know what it is like," he insisted. "I think of my sister day and night, and I will not quit searching for her until she is either found alive or laid to rest. My brother and I started this very business because of her. I was studying law, and he was dealing cards to help pay for my schooling when she boarded a train for Arizona. Her subsequent disappearance changed the course of our lives. We opened our mail-order bride business to try to ensure no other young women would suffer the way she must have suffered. To my knowledge, we're the only mail-order bride agency with a Gallant insurance clause," he bragged. "The only agency with any insurance clause, for that matter."

Olivia blinked a few times. "What sort of insurance?"

"The kind that activates a group of gallant rescuers to go

search for any bride with haste should she fail to end up at her intended destination. Or…" He raised his forefinger, "if she finds herself in distress along the way, or finds herself in an undesirable situation upon her arrival."

Miss Rothschild smiled. It was like the sun coming out from behind the clouds.

Jordan caught his breath at the way it transformed her tear-stained features from pale and bruised to something truly glorious. "We run a successful agency, I am proud to say," he continued. "In the past five years, we've placed a decent number of brides in good, solid marriages."

Her smile widened. "I don't suppose your Gallant rescuers would be willing to escort a would-be bride out of town *before* any calamities befall her?" Her voice was teasing, but her expression cautiously hopeful.

"A would-be bride," he repeated slowly. "Does that mean you've changed your mind about signing a bridal contract?" The prospect of hearing her say yes made his stomach knot like a pretzel. *Please say no.* For reasons he couldn't make sense of, he did not wish to draw up the paperwork that would transform her into yet another client. She was different, somehow. Not like the others. Extra special, though for the life of him, he couldn't say why.

"Perhaps," was her surprising reply. "If that is the only way to enlist your dratted Gallant rescuers, I might just have to consider it."

"There might be another way," he assured swiftly. It was an idea that might cause his brother to question his wits after they reached Arizona, but it was the first thing that popped into his mind. "I could escort you from town."

"You?" She shook her head in amazement. "How is that possible?" She glanced around the room. "Who would run your office here in Boston while you are away?"

He arched one dark brow at her. "I recently hired a secretary." He stood and pulled a watch piece from his pocket to glance at the time. It was nearly seven. Best to get Miss Roth-schild on her way before dark. "Though I am still training her, I assure you, Ms. Carter is more than capable of keeping me apprised of any and all important matters of business via telegram."

"In that case," Olivia Rothschild rose to her feet with a swish of silk skirts, "I accept your kind offer, sir. How soon may we depart?" She stepped around him to tuck her damp handkerchief in her woven ivory reticule. Then she tightened the drawstrings and glanced up at him expectantly.

"As soon as you are ready," he heard himself saying. *What are you? A sorceress? Egad!* All she had to do was bat her damp lashes and curve her swollen lips at him, and he was jumping to do her bidding.

Her expression brightened. "In my heart, I am more than ready. Alas, I must enlist the aid of my most faithful house-hold staff members to pack. Then there is my father's man of business to contact about a few financial matters, as well as my guardian. I fear it will take me a full twenty-four hours to accomplish everything that needs to happen before I depart."

"Your guardian." His upper lip curled in consternation. If Olivia Rothschild was not of an age to make her own deci-sions, then everything he'd just agreed to was null and void. "Will he or she be accompanying us?"

Miss Rothschild made a sound of disgust. "You would not be able to pry Beatrice Rothschild from the social whirl of the Boston elite no matter how hard you tried." She made no attempt to mask her sarcasm. "Believe me when I say Aunt Bee is my guardian on paper only. My father saw to that."

"For how much longer?" he asked, wondering exactly what she meant by possessing a "guardian on paper only." Did the minx somehow already have control over her own wealth?

"For another year," she retorted with a toss of her blonde head. The movement caused a wispy curl to spring free from its pins. It bounced in defiance against her temple.

"Making you twenty years of age." MaryAnne's exact age when she'd disappeared.

"In less than a month I will be."

He would be traveling with a nineteen-year-old? He shot to his feet. "That will never do," he growled. "Please accept my deepest apologies, Miss Rothschild, but I fear I may have to welsh on my word, after all. It would be unseemly for a man my age to escort a nineteen-year-old without a proper chaperone." He was six and twenty. In comparison, she was a mere babe.

She made a pretty little moue at him. "Never fear, Mr. Branson. I shall not be alone. Quite the contrary. I rarely go anywhere without my maid, Inga. Tonight was an exception. An emergency, if you will. And considering how far we will be traveling and how long we might be gone, I shall also bring my chef, Marceau, who will additionally insist on bringing his younger brother, Milo. He's but fifteen but a tremendously useful lad to have around." A peal of laughter escaped her. "Now that I think of it, there is a chance my man of business, Zeke Sanford, will offer to join us for at least part of the trip. He just this morning mentioned something about needing to visit a few of our midwestern subsidiaries."

Her man of business. There was a steely note of ownership in her voice that caught Jordan off guard. He hardly knew what to say. In a handful of seconds, their temporary partnership of two had grown threefold.

"About that bridal contract of yours," Miss Rothschild continued briskly. She was all business now.

"As I previously stated, a contract will not be necessary to secure my escort," he reminded. "As it turns out, I have business in Arizona." Or rather, he did now. He would be sure to introduce her to the other brides he and his brother had recently matched in Headstone — Hannah, Callie, Felicity, Meg, and Daisy. She would become his inside source of information, a source he hoped would offer some clue to MaryAnne's whereabouts...or demise.

"I wish to sign one anyway."

He nearly swallowed his tongue. "Whatever for?"

"For the added protection of your Gallant insurance clause." She shot him a cheeky smile. "Mind you, I'll be nego-tiating a few amendments to it."

I should not have expected otherwise, you little minx! Outra-geous Olivia was back in full force, tears dried and her incor-rigible spirit ready to lock horns with the world. "I see," he muttered, bracing himself.

"I will only marry if my affections are engaged." The color was high in her cheeks once more, as her blue gaze fixed challengingly on his. "A man I can trust and respect, as well."

His mouth went dry, and his collar suddenly felt too constricting. "Fair enough." It was the strangest contract he'd ever negotiated. Most of the women he placed in marriages hoped for love someday but were not expecting it right away. Then again, Olivia Rothschild wasn't most women. She apparently knew what she wanted and didn't plan to wait for it.

"If, however," she continued in a severe voice, "you fail to find a man able to engage my affections within the forth-coming three months, you will release me from my contract without question. We will part ways in Arizona, and that will be the end of it."

Three months, eh? He wondered how the indulged young debutante had come up with such a precise number. Matters of the heart took time, sometimes years to develop to full maturity. On the other hand, he'd never been given so much time to ply his trade. Three months was an eternity compared to how quickly most of his clients expected to be matched.

"Agreed," he said softly. "I'll draw up the contract in the morning. You may sign it before we depart." Why, oh why, was he so overjoyed at the prospect of having three months to place his latest bridal candidate in a marriage? It made no more sense than the excitement he felt at the knowledge he would be by her side every step of the way — teaming up in a renewed search for MaryAnne's whereabouts. Perhaps it would be best to keep that particular detail of their arrangement from his brother upon their arrival. Colt was going to be livid enough already about how he'd left their Boston office in the hands of a newly trained secretary.

"Good. Let us at least shake on it tonight." Without waiting for a response, Miss Rothschild reached for his hand.

He was so surprised by the feel of her warm fingers curling around his that he acted on pure male instinct. He laced his fingers through hers and brought her hand to his lips. "I give you my word, Miss Rothschild. I'll get you safely to Arizona. There you will help me renew my search for my sister, while I commence a search for your perfect match."

Her answering smile warmed the darkest, loneliest corners of his heart. He should have recognized it for what it was — the smile of a spoiled, indulged debutante who'd once more gotten her way.

Instead, for the first time in a very long time, he foolishly tasted hope.

CHAPTER 3: FINANCIAL SHENANIGANS

OLIVIA

"*O*ne moment, please." Mr. Branson hurried across the room to retrieve their coats. He returned and held hers up while she stepped into it. "It is growing dark outside. Allow me to drive you home."

She frowned. "I am not certain that would be entirely proper." *Heaven knows I'm in enough trouble already.* "It is best if I walk."

"Alone?" He raised his dark brows at her. "I hardly see the safeness in that. How about a compromise? I'll hire a hackney."

"A compromise it is." She smiled her gratitude at not having to make the chilly trek home on foot. "But before we go, may I trouble you for one more small favor, sir?"

He arched a brow at her with a comically distrusting expression.

She chuckled and raised her hands in surrender. "A pen and paper is all I need this time."

"Very well. Follow me." He strode to his desk and unearthed the requested materials with a frown of impatience riding his tanned features. "If I may ask, what is the urgency of this note, Miss Rothschild? Why must it be written tonight?" He centered the sheet of paper on the mahogany surface of his desk and uncapped the inkwell for her. With a wave of his hands, he ushered her into his office chair.

She chuckled again as she took a seat and reached for the pen he held out. "The urgency, my dear Mr. Branson, is the fact we will be leaving the city soon. I am requesting the necessary funds from my banker is all." She cast a sideways glance at him to gauge how close he was hovering. Too close.

"A moment of privacy, if you will?" She fluttered a hand to wave him away. There was no need for him to witness the amount she intended to withdraw, nor whose name she would endorse the request with.

He treated her to a ferocious scowl before moving to the front picture window to flip the open sign to closed. Planting his feet there, he crossed his arms and stared outside. She waited until he was a safe distance before she began to write. Signing Zeke Sanfords's name with a flourish, she waved the paper in the air to dry the ink. It was apparent that Mr. Jordan Branson was a straight arrow, as straight as they come. Not in a million years would he understand the rather convoluted arrangement she had with her man of business.

For all intents and purposes, she was going behind her aunt's back and had been doing so for some time, ever since she and Zeke had discovered Beatrice Rothschild's mountain of indiscretions. She wasn't just sorely mismanaging Olivia's finances due to her spendthrift inclinations, she was also using them to maintain an illicit affair with a younger man, an unfortunate situation that could be used to ruin both of them — permanently — if the wrong person got ahold of the juicy details. Fortunately for them all, Olivia and Zeke (at least to the best of her knowledge) were the only ones in possession of the damning information, and neither of them had any intention of letting it see the light of day. However, it gave her a certain power over her aunt when it came to their financial dealings, a power she very much enjoyed and had taken advantage of in recent months.

Alas, kissing Alec Grenville had transferred some of that hard-won power back to her aunt. The woman was as thick as thieves with the aging Mr. Grenville, Alec's great-uncle. It was very possible — terrifyingly so — that she'd already made some sort of deal with him about her niece's nuptials to his nephew. A fortune as large as the Rothschild's naturally attracted any number of unscrupulous plots and machinations. Her father had warned her of this before his passing. It was the very reason he'd appointed Zeke Sanford as the sole trustee over her fortune and all attached business dealings, making it impossible for her aunt to do much without his signature and authority.

"What now, Miss Rothschild?" Jordan Branson's low baritone jolted her from her reverie. "You look as if you've caught sight of a new pack of trouble heading your way."

What an accurate summation of my predicament! Amazed, and a wee bit disturbed by his razor-sharp intuition, she forced another cheery smile to her lips. "The bank is closed for the evening, but I happen to be aware the president spends his Friday evenings at the Irish Brew Pub on 5th Avenue. Would you be so kind as to transport me there, Mr. Branson? It is on our way."

He rolled his eyes at her, but motioned her forward with the flick of a wrist. "Why do I suddenly feel like your accomplice, Miss Rothschild?" Without waiting for an answer, he ushered her out the front door and locked it behind them.

She suppressed the urge to shiver at the imprint of his long fingers gently gripping her elbow. Unlike the young bucks across Boston who pursued her relentlessly for her fortune, all the while scoffing at its origins, Mr. Branson simply treated her like a lady. He'd not once broached the topic of her finances throughout the hour they'd been conversing. No subtle hints. No thinly cloaked jibes. In fact, the entire focus of their conversation had remained on her current dilemma and how he could assist her. Well, they'd deviated briefly to a discussion about his long-lost sister, but that was it.

Twilight stretched across the heavens as they stood on the busy cobblestone curb outside the Boomtown Mail Order Brides Company. Hackneys and wagons rumbled past, as well as an occasional stagecoach. Olivia glanced over her shoulder at his office building one last time, hardly believing she'd darkened the door of a bridal agency. Her dearly departed parents were likely turning in their graves over the fact.

She didn't even want to contemplate her Aunt Beatrice's reaction if she found out, either, not that it would matter a day from now. She would soon be many miles away from Boston, the unwitting kiss she'd given Alec Grenville, and her former best friend's spiteful spreading of the sordid tale.

"Cold?" Mr. Branson's concerned voice wafted over her. His gloved hands reached out to button her fur collar beneath her chin. "There. Is that better?"

She nodded, grinning. "Do you always cluck over your clients like a mother hen?"

Instead of answering, he waved down a hackney and lifted her inside.

This time she was unable to suppress a shiver at the steely strength of his hands on her waist. She watched him from beneath her lashes while he removed his top hat. As he hefted his tall frame through the doorway, a gust of wind ruffled his dark hair, sending an errant lock sliding down on his forehead. Her fingers immediately itched to smooth it from his face. She curled her hand into a fist and tried to think of something else.

Which was difficult since Mr. Branson opted to leave the seat empty across from her. Instead, he claimed the cushion next to her and stretched out his long legs in front of him with a sigh.

She continued to discreetly study him as he rested his top hat on the far side of their seat, unbuttoned his black overcoat, and allowed it to slide open. Unless she was mistaken, there was the bulge of a handgun beneath his black silk waistcoat.

"You're armed," she observed curiously.

"A necessity in my line of business." He tipped his head back against the seat and closed his eyes. "A precaution against any evil that might befall my lovely clientele, something I have thankfully never had to employ." He cracked one eyelid open and trained a piercing look on her. "Please do not change those statistics this evening, Miss Rothschild."

She sniffed in affront. "I am merely paying a visit to my banker, sir."

"After hours," he pointed out, closing his eyes once more. "At an establishment where he is likely engaged in a game of cards."

Oh, I am counting on it. She smiled at her disgruntled escort in the deepening shadows. If the rumors were true, the president of the Central Avenue Bank had recently taken out a loan to cover a gambling debt.

To her delight, said rumors proved to be true indeed, which meant Olivia had no trouble using the information as leverage to lead the blustering, balding man back to their hackney. He flung himself down in the seat across from her and Mr. Branson, clearly put out at being wrested so abruptly from his game.

Considering that he'd been sorely losing, she felt like she

had done him a rollicking good turn. "The bank on Central Avenue," she sweetly informed their driver. To the bank president, she simpered, "It is so kind of you to accommodate my request after hours, Mr. Putney. What with my rush to leave town and all, I am most grateful."

"Seeing as you're so generously compensating me for my trouble," he growled, "how could I refuse?"

You could not afford to, poor fellow. It was all part of my plan. She nodded at him and lapsed into silence for the duration of their short ride to the bank. When the team of horses drew to a halt, she laid a hand on Mr. Branson's forearm. "We shall remain here, you and I. Mr. Putney does not require our assistance."

Mr. Branson's hand came down on the top of hers the moment the door slammed shut behind Mr. Putney. "This is the part where you apprise me of what is truly going on here." His eyes were wide open now.

She treated him to an innocent smile. "A simple bank withdrawal, sir." Albeit a sizable one. Eight hundred dollars to be precise.

His fingers tightened on hers. "From your own accounts, correct? I wouldn't mind a little assurance I am not aiding and abetting a bank robbery this evening." He waited until she lifted her startled gaze to his. "Though you would make a very lovely bank robber, come to think of it."

"I am not robbing a bank," she snapped. "How can you ask such a thing? I know we've just become acquainted, but you are surely a better judge of character than that. Not to mention, we are about to become traveling companions for the next several days. Under the circumstances, you might consider the merits of at least pretending to be pleasant."

"I am pleasant." His offered her a maddening smile. "Always. It is a job requirement, Miss Rothschild."

She suppressed another shiver that had nothing whatsoever to do with the temperature in the air as she stared back. Somehow, during their drive from the brew pub to the bank, Mr. Branson's visage had grown more intriguing. Perhaps it was the shadows falling around them, or perhaps it was the knowing, half-amused glint to his dark gaze; but Olivia was suddenly very much aware she was no longer dealing with the foolish young bucks of Boston's social elite.

Mr. Branson was different from the young men in her circle. He was older, for one thing. More seasoned. More mature. One second he was blustering over her tearful self like a concerned parent, and the next moment he was holding her captive with his all-seeing, all-knowing gaze.

Though, at the moment, there was nothing parental in the way he was studying her. It made her insides all aflutter to be alone with him in such a small, enclosed space. Even so, she appreciated the fact he made no move to take advantage of their proximity. The hard set to his jawline indicated he was very much in control, an iron-clad control she wouldn't mind testing at some point.

Now where had that thought come from? Olivia felt the heat rise to her cheeks. She was grateful for the shadows and for the fact her thoughts were one of the few things that were safe from Mr. Branson.

Something told her she would never be able to bamboozle him the way she'd done with her guardian on so many occasions. He was wiser, more discerning. The thought both thrilled and scared her. It was as if she'd finally met her match.

"Tell me," the object of her musings instructed in a low, gravelly tone. "Who is forcing you to marry a man against your will? It will be easier to protect you in the coming days if I better understand the threat."

She made a face. He already knew about her nickname and her dubious reputation. He might as well know the full truth. "My aunt wishes for me to marry Alec Grenville." Perhaps, "wishes" wasn't the right word for the dire warnings and threats Aunt Bee had spewed on her earlier.

"The marquis' cousin?" His brows rose. "Why his cousin? Every other hopeful mama has her sights set on the marquis, himself."

"As did my aunt," she confessed in a small voice. "Until I bungled her plans by kissing the wrong man." She glanced away, unable to continue meeting Mr. Branson's curious gaze.

"You did what?"

His incredulous tone raised her hackles. "I kissed Alec Grenville," she spat. "I thought I was following my aunt's instructions. I had no idea he was pretending to be his cousin for the evening. They look a lot alike, you know."

"What right have you to be angry at their antics? You were the one trying to entrap a man into marriage." The outraged snarl in his voice was unmistakable. "I think I am beginning to understand how well deserved your title is, Outrageous Olivia."

"I was," she admitted. "And it isn't something I am particularly proud of. It's just that I've been trying so hard to please my aunt — to be the stylish and lauded debutante she wants me so badly to be that I lost sight of who I really am." A woman of integrity like her parents had raised her to be. The thought made her want to start weeping all over again.

"And that is?" Mr. Branson's tone was still stiff but no longer as censorious.

"A woman who regretted the kiss the moment it happened." She bit her lower lip, recalling Alec's cold lips and the hard way he'd ground them against hers. "It was my first time." She sniffed damply. "It was supposed to be beautiful, precious, and memorable, but..." It was memorable, alright, but not in the way she'd imagined. Such was the consequence of kissing a man she did not love for all the wrong reasons.

"Did he force himself on you?" Mr. Branson asked coldly, straightening in his seat.

"Oh, no!" she assured quickly. "It was entirely my fault for tempting him. Aunt Bee insisted I wear a low-cut gown when he came calling. Then she refused to allow Inga to accompany us on our drive. It's no wonder he saw me as ripe for the plucking. What is worse, it happened in plain view of, well, a good number of our friends." She ducked her head in mortification at the recollection. "And in that moment, I realized I had become someone I did not wish to be. A daughter my parents would no longer recognize if they were still here." Her breathing hitched. "That is the real reason I am leaving town, sir. If you no longer wish to accompany me, I will understand. Nevertheless, I am leaving," she concluded in a harder voice.

Mr. Branson's hand remained resting atop hers. "I am a man of my word, Miss Rothschild. I said I would accompany you to Arizona, and accompany you I will."

A fresh flood of grateful tears swam in her eyes, but he was no longer looking at her. He was watching the stocky figure of Mr. Putney rush down the stairs of the bank, carrying a small black travel bag.

Right before the banker flung open the hackney door, Mr. Branson let go of her hand. He leaned forward and reached for the travel bag, presumably to make it easier for Mr. Putney to climb aboard.

"That won't be necessary, sir." The bank president waved away his hand. Before returning to his seat across from them, he handed the bag to her. "As you requested, Miss Rothschild."

She gave him a tight smile. "My companion is armed, so I

am only going to ask this question one time. Is it all accounted for?"

He nodded vehemently, backing away from her and sinking heavily into his seat. "Every last dollar of it, I assure you, ma'am." He removed his hat, fumbled for his handkerchief, and used it to wipe his sweaty brow.

"Minus your payment, of course," she pressed.

"Yes, indeed. I counted it three times. It is accurate to the penny." He mopped his brow a second time.

She didn't bother opening the travel bag. The pitiful man was trembling. He was telling the truth. "Your home address," she demanded in a low voice. "We are taking you there. I've every intention of seeing that your payment for tonight's transaction makes it home to your wife and children. I'll not stand for my hard-earned money being wasted on yet another deck of cards."

"Yes, Miss Rothschild. Of course, Miss Rothschild." The bank president bobbed his head again and babbled out his home address.

In short order, their driver had him deposited on the curb of his fancy townhome and was once more rolling in the direction of the home down the street she shared with her Aunt Bee.

Jordan Branson's amused gaze met hers as the hackney came to a stop before the entry gates. "Well, Miss Rothschild, if the last few hours are any indication, escorting you to Arizona is going to be the most entertainment I've had in years."

She made a face at him. "I am glad my troubles have provided you so much amusement."

"Not your troubles. You, Miss Rothschild. You might've been kissed against your will and nearly forced into marriage earlier this afternoon, but such events in no way dimmed your fighting spirit."

"Oh?" she shot him a puzzled look. "So you don't consider me to be an utterly deplorable, unredeemable creature after the kiss? A kiss I will from now on refer to as the Grenville incident." She shivered in revulsion.

"Far from it. In fact, I find the way you delivered Mr. Putney to his doorstep with his earnings in hand was a kind and charitable thing to do. Though I must confess, it was entertaining the way you had him jumping like a bullfrog at the sound of your voice." He shook his head, voice growing quieter. "I heard you were a force to be reckoned with, Miss Rothschild. The rumors were not exaggerated."

There was a gentleness to his expression that unnerved her to the point of making her knees feel weak. And his words? They were like a ray of warm sunlight on a cold, winter day. "Thank you, Mr. Branson."

He nodded and reached around her to open the hackney door. "One more thing, Miss Rothschild. As the co-owner of a mail-order bride agency, I feel honor bound to assure you of this." He waited until she met his gaze squarely before continuing. "Someday you are going to kiss a man you truly care for, and his kiss will make you forget Alec Grenville ever existed."

She felt her lashes grow damp again. "Do you really mean that, Mr. Branson?" His compassion was so unexpected, she couldn't think of anything more profound to say. She'd fully expected his censure when she'd confided how badly she'd besmirched her reputation. His disdain.

"I make a habit of only saying things I mean, Miss Roth-schild," he returned dryly. After another intense and searching look that rendered her breathless, he opened the door and leaped from their hackney. Then he turned and reached for her.

Trying not to think about how strong and steady his arms were as he assisted her to the ground, she carefully averted her face. He was way too clever and observant for her peace of mind; and she very much did *not* wish for him to deduce her current thoughts. They were still on the topic of kissing, but not just kissing in general. She was specifically imagining what it would be like to kiss him!

CHAPTER 4: GATHERING STORM

JORDAN

*A*t precisely twenty-four hours after Jordan delivered Miss Rothschild to her aunt's glamorous townhome, a rather impressive caravan of carriages drew alongside the curb outside his office. He'd sent Ms. Carter home two hours earlier but had remained in the agency to complete some final paperwork in preparation for his upcoming trip to Arizona.

Puzzled at the commotion taking place outside, he left his desk and moved to stand before the tall picture window. In the twilight, he determined there were five carriages in total, all of them piled as high as humanly possible with trunks, travel bags, and other bundles. His mind quickly raced over the possibilities. There was an empty shop two doors down. Perhaps, a new business owner had purchased or rented it.

He watched as the driver of the first carriage hopped down with alacrity to fling the passenger door wide for its occupants. His jaw dropped as Miss Rothschild emerged in a stylish travel hat dripping with peacock feathers, a striking gown of royal blue silk, and a mink edged cloak. It took considerable effort to maneuver her full skirts through the opening. When the toes of her dainty boots at last touched the ground, she was swiftly joined by the occupants of the other carriages.

There were four individuals in all. Her personal maid, Inga, was the easiest to pick out, because she was the only other woman. She was a round woman with cheery features, wearing a simple gray gown and white apron. Her chestnut hair so thick it was held in place by a snood. Marceau and Milo were equally easy to pick out from the small group, because they looked so French and so very much alike. Milo was a fifteen-year-old version of his older brother who served as Olivia's chef. Like Inga, they were wearing uniforms, mostly black, though they sported white dress shirts beneath their vests emblazoned with a family crest — the Rothschild crest, he presumed.

Jordan had no idea who the third man was, but he was determined to find out with haste. Striding to the front door, he threw it open and stood scowling at his late-evening callers.

"Mr. Branson!" Miss Rothschild breezed. "I was so hoping we would arrive in time to catch you still at your office. Otherwise, I would not have known exactly where to find you." She glided in his direction with dark gloved hands outstretched as if they were old friends.

Against his better judgment, he took her hands. Instead of shaking them or raising them to his lips in the manner of a perfect gentleman, he held them fast, squeezing them lightly to get her full attention.

Her blue gaze turned cautious, though her perfect pink lips continued to smile at him.

He dropped his voice and darted a glance in both directions. "What are you doing here at such a late hour, Miss Rothschild? For a young woman who is supposed to be striving to repair a damaged reputation, I fail to understand how being seen alone with me at this hour…"

She rolled her eyes but lowered her voice to match his. "La, Mr. Branson. Do not be such a drudge. I promised to return in twenty-fours, and my word is good. I am ready to depart. I hope you can say the same for yourself, sirrah!" she cajoled.

"Tonight?" His hands tightened on hers. "You expect us to begin our journey west this very evening?" It was a preposterous suggestion, born of years of spoiled indulgence. Clearly, the chit had no concept how things worked in the real world.

"Zeke," she commanded in a low, cultured voice, without turning her head. "If you will produce our tickets, I believe it will put Mr. Branson's mind at ease."

Zeke. His brows rose at the mention of the man's name. *As in Zeke Sanford?* "You brought your father's man of business, as well?"

She gave her head a careless toss, making the peacock feathers on her hat bounce. "I am not bringing him, per se. He offered outright to accompany us. He has business out of town with a few subsidiaries of ours and will be traveling in our general direction. There was no reason whatsoever for him not to join our party. Do you not agree?" She playfully arched her blonde brows at him.

Before he could respond, Mr. Sanford stepped forward in his shiny black boots and tall top hat to hand him a strip of paper. "Your train ticket, sir. To repay your kindness in escorting her and her companions to Arizona, Miss Rothschild insisted on covering the expense." He inclined his head as he held out the ticket. "I am Zeke Sanford, manager of operations at Rothschild Industries. A pleasure to meet you, sir." He cast a speaking look at the way Jordan's hands still held his mistress's captive.

Embarrassed beyond measure at his indiscretion, he immediately dropped the delicate appendages. "I am likewise pleased to make your acquaintance." He held out his hand to Mr. Sanford, and with the other accepted the train ticket. "Jordan Branson, owner of the Boomtown Mail Order Brides Company."

Mr. Sanford's hazel gaze mirrored a dozen questions, but he politely kept his peace while Jordan examined the ticket.

"Our train leaves in an hour." He waved the offending scrap of paper at its lovely purchaser. "What's the meaning of this?" He was packed already, but he saw no sense in fleeing town like a fugitive instead of waiting until morning after a good night's sleep.

Her laughing demeanor evaporated. "So much for my attempts to approach our journey in the light of a grand new adventure." She sighed. "Since you insist on continuing to throw a wet blanket on my fun, I have no choice but to confess the urgency of my departure has increased in recent hours." She threw such a fearful glance over her shoulder that he followed her gaze.

He detected nothing out of the ordinary taking place on the street beyond them — nothing, that is, beyond her rather extraordinary gathering of staff members and belongings.

"My aunt spent the better part of the day with the Grenvilles, negotiating my forthcoming nuptials to the loathsome Alec. She is holed up with him in his office as we stand here conversing, writing out the bans they will post on the morrow. Please, Mr. Branson." She tipped her face up to his and trained beseeching blue eyes on him. "If I am to leave town unhindered, now is my best window of opportunity." When he didn't immediately respond, she pressed. "I am leaving, sir, with or without you, though I much prefer to have you by my side."

I much prefer to have you by my side. What she was asking

of him was, perhaps, the most foolish, ill-advised action he had ever taken. He was a grown man. He had no right to involve himself in the personal affairs of a wealthy heiress.

He shook his head. "Without your aunt's permission," he mused quietly. It would be morally wrong, if not criminal, to aid her flight out of town while her guardian was right now penning her wedding contract to Alec Grenville. It would be a binding and legal document in the eyes of the law.

"I have Zeke Sanford's permission," she snapped. "If you will but produce the contract you stated you were preparing this morning, we will sign it with haste and be on our way."

He frowned down at her, wishing things were as simple as she pretended they were. He pitied her situation; he truly did, but it was out of his hands unless she could provide a convincing new reason for them to continue with their original plan. "I do not understand how Mr. Sanford's permission bears any weight on the matter. Please elaborate, Miss Rothschild."

She pouted at him. "I recall explaining to you yesterday how my father was careful to make his sister my guardian on paper only. He didn't fully trust her, you see. He knew how frivolous and flighty she could be, a social butterfly and spendthrift. Alas, she was all the family we had left, so he had little choice but to include her in his legacy on his deathbed. Fortunately, Zeke holds the real power over my wellbeing, finances, and affairs. My father made him, not Aunt Bee, the sole trustee over my accounts. She can fuss and make demands of him all she wishes, but in the end, she can only access the funds he authorizes."

Outrage surged in Jordan's chest at the picture her words created. If everything she said was to be believed, she'd been living at the mercy of an unscrupulous aunt these past several years, a woman who might very well have concocted the whole Alec Grenville scheme for the sole purpose of getting her grasping hands on yet more of the Rothschild fortune. He could imagine any number of secret bargains being made by her in the dark with the Grenvilles. Even if she demanded payment upfront from them for delivering her niece over to them like a sacrifice on a platter, they would come out the winners once Olivia's fortune passed to her new husband.

Jordan clenched his jaw. His own integrity and dignity demanded he not stand by and witness something so deplorable taking place beneath his very nose. Trying to convince himself it had nothing to do with his personal abhorrence to the thought of Olivia Rothschild being married to someone else, he dragged in a bracing breath of air. "So, technically, your aunt is within her legal right to negotiate a marriage contract for you?"

"Yes, but not for long." Miss Rothschild paused and bit her lower lip as if debating how much to tell him. "Zeke just this afternoon procured a sworn statement from my aunt's lover. A confession, if you will. If produced in court, this document will provide convincing evidence Aunt Bee was in no moral or fit state of mind to make such an arrangement on her behalf. It is all there in the confession. The funds she has spent on their little nest where they hold their trysts. The monthly allowance she provided him, from *my* accounts, no less!" She bit off her words in disgust. The color was high in her cheeks, and her slender frame vibrated with agitation.

Zeke Sanders laid a comforting hand on her arm. "Never fear. It is my professional opinion, the document will hold up in court, Miss Rothschild."

"And bring about complete ruin for both her and I in the process," she mourned. "I'll never be able to set foot in Boston again if word of her indiscretions gets out. We'll be banned from all respectable establishments." She patted his hand and bestowed such a pleading look on him that Jordan's insides clenched in protest. "It is far better I leave town. My absence will greatly slow my aunt's plans for me. And with a little luck, we might avoid a showdown in court altogether."

Jordan seriously doubted that was the case, but he couldn't argue the point that it was more urgent than ever to whisk Miss Rothschild to safety, at least until they had the time to form a proper legal defense for her. He suddenly wished he'd been able to finish his own law studies. If such were the case, he wouldn't have hesitated to offer to represent her. Instead, her future would rest in the hands of others.

"Felicity Barra!" he exclaimed, snapping his fingers in the air as a thought struck him. "I recently placed a mail-order bride in Headstone, Arizona. She happens to be an attorney, a good one. Perhaps, you might engage her services upon your arrival into town."

"A female attorney?" Miss Rothschild's anxious expression brightened. "How intriguing! I can't wait to make her acquaintance." She clasped her hands beneath her chin. "Well, then, Mr. Branson. I suppose the last order of business for this evening is entirely up to you. Will you or will you not be joining us at the train depot?" She glanced at Zeke, who still had a hand resting on her arm.

"Within the hour," the man added with a decided nod. His olive features were drawn with concern as he returned his attention to Jordan. "We must be on our way shortly, sir."

Jordan tried not to take offense at the possessive way the man was hovering over his client. Blast it all, but he was one of those unusual creatures whose age was hard to determine. Not only were his eyes partially hidden beneath the brim of his top hat, the falling shadows around them did nothing to expose the man's visage. One thing was for certain, he wasn't near as old as Jordan had originally supposed. If he had to venture a guess, he'd place the man in his late thirties or early forties. Compared to his own twenty-six years, that might seem old to some folks; but young heiresses were known to ally themselves with much older men at times. He could only hope and pray it wasn't the case between her and Mr. Sanford.

"My two bags are packed." His gaze flickered to Miss Rothschild and held for an extended moment. "I've never required more than two bags, madam."

She gave a tinkling laugh. "Good gracious, Mr. Branson! You can scold me all the way to Arizona, if you desire. Just please take Milo with you and hurry back with your baggage."

He did, and they were soon on their way to the train station, with her mail-order bride contract freshly signed and rolled up in his breast pocket. She bade him to join her and Zeke Sanford in the front carriage, while her hired help filed inside the second carriage. To his irritation, Mr. Sanford took the seat next to her, leaving him no choice but to settle down across from them.

"I've never made a trip quite like this one," she mused as the carriages rolled along. "I am aware I am bringing an exorbitant amount of luggage, but you can hardly blame me if you think hard enough about it. Unlike you, Mr. Branson, I have no idea what lies before me, whom I shall marry, and if I shall ever return to Boston. It seemed safest to go prepared for any number of scenarios."

Whom I shall marry... Something twisted in his gut at her words. She was trusting him to aid her in her endeavor to find a husband. As much as the prospect of placing her in a marriage troubled him, he was both contractually bound and honor bound to do right by her. To hunt, with all sincerity, for her perfect match upon their arrival to Arizona.

He nodded in the hopes of setting her at ease. "I find no reason to scold you quite all the way to Arizona, Miss Rothschild, but five carriages! I trust you've made arrangements for the secure transport of so many belongings?"

She treated him to a grin so full of life and mischief, he found himself utterly entranced. "But, of course! Zeke took care of everything. We shall have two private cars in which to travel in comfort, as well as two additional cars reserved for the overflow of our cargo. What a worry bug you are turning out to be, Mr. Branson," she added in a teasing voice. "You are beginning to remind me of my father."

His startled gaze clashed with her incorrigible one and held for an extended moment. *Her father, eh?* He reckoned he deserved that set-down with the way he'd been blustering over her affairs the entire day and a half they'd known each other. However, he was unprepared for the giant blast of protest that careened through his chest. *No!* The emotion was so acute, it took a powerful effort not to raise his hand and press it to his heart. He wasn't certain about a lot of things at the exact moment, but he was certain about one thing. He did not wish for Olivia Rothschild to regard him as a father figure. Quite the contrary.

The thought formed in his mind and took preposterous shape. What if he courted her, himself? There were a dozen or more impediments, not the least of which was her possession of a king's fortune. It was way too bad she wasn't lighter in the purse. That would have made their courtship easier. Perhaps there was a way Zeke could maintain his role as trustee and thereby avoid the whole confounded prospect of anyone viewing him, Jordan Branson, as taking advantage of a client in his care.

Because he'd gone and fallen for the minx — her laugh, her smile, her sparkling gaze, her intelligence, her wit, her unquenchable bravery in the face of such dire circumstances, and her undying optimism. She wasn't merely the spoiled indulged debutant she appeared on the surface. He surveyed her lavishly expensive gown and the very real gems winking from a necklace at her throat and experienced his first real spurt of fear on her behalf. It was through no doing and no fault of her own that she'd been born into wealth. Already, several dastardly individuals were scheming to rid her of it at the expense of her happiness and wellbeing. She deserved better, so much better than the rotten hand she'd been dealt.

His thoughts flew back to his attempt at giving her words of comfort the evening before. *Someday you are going to kiss a man you truly care for, and his kiss will make you forget Alec Grenville ever existed.* He wanted to be that man, he wanted to deliver that kiss, and he wanted it to erase the thought of every other man on the planet, including Zeke Sanford. He had no idea if her man of business would present any competition, but he intended to win her in the end, regardless.

He would wait until they were safely on the train and chugging their way westward. Then he would commence his wooing of the delectable Olivia Rothschild, the only young woman who'd ever crawled this far under his skin and stayed there. The only young woman he'd ever lost sleep over. The only young woman who'd ever talked him into doing so many foolish things in the course of a single twenty-four-hour period.

There would be hell to pay upon their arrival into Headstone. His brother, Colt, would raise a thousand protests over their match, but his mind was made up. He was going to court and wed Olivia Rothschild, if she would have him.

CHAPTER 5: PERILOUS JOURNEY

OLIVIA

*O*livia kept up the light chatter she'd learned as a proper debutante in order to keep Inga, Marceau, Milo, Zeke, and (she hoped) Mr. Branson properly entertained. She commented on the weather, the loveliness of their two private cars, and how fortunate they were to secure such comfortable accommodations on short notice. All the while, she kept a careful eye on the surrounding roads, lest the Grenvilles or her Aunt Bee come flying across town to fetch her home. She also kept an increasingly stressed eye on the train depot staff as they hustled to load her enormous pile of trunks, travel bags, and small items of furniture. Maybe it was foolish of her to arrive at the depot so heavy laden when she should have been more concerned about beating a hasty departure. However, she truly feared she might not ever be able to return to Boston, and there were a few dear items she simply could not part with, if such was the case.

Among her treasures was her mother's writing desk, a small cherry-wood cabinet with a mysterious array of drawers which happened to include two hidden compartments. She'd also been unable to part with her mother's tabletop jewelry armoire, a hand-carved piece imported from the Black Forest. Then there was her parents' prized grandfather clock, also from the Black Forest, that they had custom made to grace a narrow wall in the entry foyer. No doubt her aunt would immediately notice its disappearance, not only because of the empty spot in the hall, but also because its Winchester chimes would no longer be ringing out the hours. She was counting on the fact her aunt would accurately deduce who had taken it and not attempt to fill a burglary report. Regardless, it was a risk she was willing to take.

Not until the last bundle was loaded did Olivia breathe a sigh of relief. "We're off," she muttered, spinning around to duck inside her private travel car. She came into contact with something dark and solid.

"Oomph!" she exclaimed, reaching out with both hands to regain her balance. She found her palms resting against none other than Mr. Branson's waistcoat.

Two strong hands gripped her shoulders. "Miss Roth-schild! Are you quite alright? My deepest apologies for step-ping in your path. I did not anticipate you turning around so quickly."

He sounded so distressed she forgave him on the spot, which did nothing to calm the fierce pounding of her heart. "I am, sir. Thanks to you for catching me." She gave a breathy chuckle. "Next time, I'd better watch where I am going." They were standing so close, all she would have to do was rise on her tiptoes and lean in a few inches to press that kiss she'd been daydreaming about against his firm lips.

His dark eyes bored into hers, searching, it seemed, the depths of her very soul. "You mustn't keep looking at me that way," she said shakily.

"What?" he teased. "Like the concerned father you

accused me of behaving like earlier?" His upper lip twisted sardonically.

Oh, dear me, no! How could she have ever claimed such a thing? There was nothing fatherly about the admiring glint in his eyes and nothing whatsoever daughter-like about the responding rush of heat to her cheeks. "All I meant was, you worry too much." It was a lame response but all she could muster while her heart was racing and her lungs seemed unable to fill themselves properly with air.

"Ah, yes." His long fingers left her shoulders to curl beneath her elbows. "What was the other thing you called me? I believe it was a worry bug."

She started to lower her arms to her sides but paused when her fingers slid over the bulge against his ribs. It was a handgun secreted on his person; she was certain of it. "Yes, a worry bug." She tapped the suspicious bulge. "If all your fussing and blustering wasn't proof enough, I believe this item is. You are armed again, sir."

"I am." The smile left his face. "I have precious cargo to protect." His gaze didn't leave hers. He wasn't referring to her travel bags or furniture. It was clear he was referring to her.

She was thankful for the deepening shadows of dusk as the train gave its warning hoot it was about to take off.

Mr. Branson tucked her hand through the crook of his arm and finished escorting her inside the car she would be sharing with Inga. It was a sumptuous galley with a dining area on one end, a narrow parlor in the middle, and a bedroom suite at the far end, just like she'd ordered. Though she'd yet to take a tour of it, there was also a much smaller compartment off from her bedchamber that contained a bunk for Inga. Her maid was fluttering about the kitchenette adjoining the dining area with its ornate high-back, cushioned chairs.

Olivia gave a delighted sniff at the aroma of orange and spices. "It appears Inga is making us a pot of tea." She squeezed his arm. "Oh, do stay for a spell, Mr. Branson. It's not very late, and I would enjoy the company." She spoiled the lighthearted request with a shiver of cold and fear. The truth was, she wasn't ready to part with her armed companion until they safely pulled away from the Boston depot.

To her relief, Mr. Branson was in an amicable mood. "I confess I have a great weakness for tea, Miss Rothschild. Teas of every flavor from every continent. It's not a very manly drink in comparison to whiskey or port. Nevertheless, it is my drink of choice."

She sniffed. "Morally, it's the better choice, sir." She fully approved of his tastebuds for tea. There were enough Alec Grenvilles in the world consuming stiffer beverages.

"I'm glad you approve, Miss Rothschild." The amused smile he gave her made her toes curl in her boots. La, but the man possessed such a delicious smile! Enough to make most of the debutantes of her acquaintance swoon. He was unaccountably handsome, too. He didn't have the smooth baby face of the dashing young bucks in her social whirl. Instead, his tanned jawline had a swarthier cast due to his evening shadow; and there were tiny crinkle lines around his eyes as if he smiled often, which she imagined he did in his line of business. He was older than most of her comrades, more mature, and, well, just…more.

The train beneath their feet began to move. It gave another few toots as they chugged away from the station. Olivia glanced out the window, happy to see they were departing Boston at last. *Good riddance!*

She returned her attentions to Mr. Branson, and her heart gave one of those flutters it always gave when she was in his presence. As they settled down on the velvet sofa in the sitting area, she glanced around for her manager of operations, but he was absent at the moment. "Have you seen Zeke?" She worriedly eyed the door to the short walkway connecting their two cars.

"He is assisting Marceau and Milo with getting our space arranged for sleeping. There are two bunks in the back, but apparently Marceau objects to small, enclosed spaces. He begged to sleep on the couch. Mr. Sanford is currently attempting to convince both brothers to take his chamber, instead. He says he doesn't mind small spaces and would be happy to sleep on one of the bunks."

"Thank you for humoring my chef." Olivia smiled at the ease and nonchalance in which Mr. Branson reported the goings-on in his train car. He didn't seem the least bit perturbed about the shenanigans of her staff, nor did he appear to have any expectation of her to step in and administer discipline. "Marceau can be difficult at times, but he more than makes up for it in the kitchen." She was happy to tolerate his occasional quirk of temperament for such. He and his brother were otherwise hardworking, honest, respectful, and loyal.

"I look forward to proving you right." Mr Branson's dark eyes twinkled merrily at her. "It is not often a bachelor like myself gets to travel in such luxury with a hostess as lovely as you, and the promise of superb cuisine to top it all off."

You think I'm lovely? Perhaps he was simply being charming? Perhaps he dribbled compliments like chocolate syrup on all his bridal candidates? Regardless, her heartbeat sped so rapidly at his words that it made her feel lightheaded. And tongue-tied. Fortunately, Inga came to her rescue by delivering their teacups.

"I thank you, Inga." She reached gratefully for the cup and raised it to her lips for the first glorious sip. She closed her eyes and allowed the soothing scent of orange and spices to tease her senses. Gracious, but Inga could make a pot of tea like no other!

"You like it, Miss Olivia?" her maid asked anxiously. "It is a new blend. I've not brewed it before."

Olivia opened her eyelids. "It is delicious," she assured. "The perfect start to our journey." It was a good omen. Though the circumstances under which she was leaving Boston weren't ideal, there was no reason she couldn't enjoy the train ride, itself. It would provide a few days reprieve before the hailstorm of lawsuits began. Not to mention she would have the brave and dashing Mr. Branson at her side. What could possibly go wrong?

A good number of things could go wrong, as it turned out.

AN AUTUMN STORM blew their way on the second day of their journey, filling their ears with thunder and turning their vision to stars with blinding blasts of lightning. Even after the rain subsided, the skies remained gray, making it impossible to read without a lantern. The overcast skies also made it difficult to play chess or charades, two of Olivia's favorite forms of entertainment.

On the third day, their train developed a mechanical problem and was forced to remain several extra hours at the next station. Olivia was on pins and needles the entire afternoon. She wasn't far enough away from Boston yet. Any major delays could give the Grenvilles and her aunt time to catch up with her. Thankfully, the afternoon passed without incident, the train was repaired, and they set off once more.

The fourth day of their journey brought about Zeke Sanford's first stop.

"I am coming with you," Olivia announced in a voice that

brooked no protests. She, Zeke, and Mr. Branson were seated at her dining table, having just enjoyed a breakfast repast of peppered quiche "The schedule says we will be here more than two hours. That should be more than enough time for a round-trip to our subsidiary."

"I've no objections." Zeke nodded approvingly. "You've a good head for business. Besides, I would enjoy the company."

"May I accompany you, as well, Mr. Sanford?"

Olivia glanced in surprise across the table at Mr. Branson and discovered him staring darkly at Zeke. *What in heaven's name has Zeke ever done to offend you?*

ZEKE SANFORD RUBBED a hand over his freshly shaven jawline. "Call me Zeke, please. We are traveling in too close of quarters to stand on ceremony." He pursed his lips. "Are you interested in learning more about shipping, Mr. Branson?"

"If I agree to drop the mister, then you must, too. I much prefer being called Jordan." His shoulders relaxed a fraction. Though he was prepared to dislike Zeke on the sole grounds they might be in competition for Miss Rothschild's affections, he was turning out to be an unusually likable fellow.

Zeke nodded his assent.

Jordan tried to choose his words carefully. "No, I am not particularly interested in learning about shipping or trade, other than what I read in the newspaper. But because of the marriage contract you signed, naturally I am interested in learning everything there is to learn about Miss Rothschild." It would never do to admit his true reason — serving as chaperone to the two of them. He detested the thought of them spending even an hour alone together. Out of the corner of his eye, he noted her cheeks turning pink.

"That is understandable." Zeke's expression was approving. "And I appreciate your honesty. Many a young bounder has feigned interest in shipping merely to worm his way farther into my client's good graces."

"Oh, for pity's sake!" she exploded. "Stop speaking as if I am not sitting right here. And may we dispense with formalities altogether? I am beyond weary of being called Miss Rothschild."

His brows rose. "I did not wish to appear impertinent on such short acquaintance, ma'am."

She scowled at him. "Olivia. Not Miss. Not ma'am. Not madam. You have agreed to find a husband for me, for pity's sake. I think that puts us well past formalities."

He stared for a moment, wondering for the life of him what he found so enchanting about her. Even when she was berating him, he wanted nothing more than to haul her into his arms and plant a kiss square on her sassy lips. "Very well. From now on, Olivia and Jordan it shall be." It was his turn to feel the heat creep up his neck. *Olivia and Jordan.* Pairing their names together thus sounded so marvelous. So right.

"And, yes. You may go with us." Olivia rolled her eyes at Zeke. "Our matchmaker is armed," she confided in a loud whisper to Zeke.

He looked a bit sheepish. "I reckon I should be, too. I've just never had a steady enough hand at the shooting range. Always feared I would do more harm than good in a gun fight."

"Then it's settled." Jordan patted the hidden firearm tucked against his chest. "I will lend you my protection today, which I hope we will not need."

Zeke chuckled. "I believe the train is slowing at last. Let us prepare for our rendezvous with the crotchety owner of Milligan Subsidiaries."

THE THREE OF them set off on foot down Main Street since Brim Milligan's warehouses were conveniently adjacent to the train depot.

"The name Brim has an interesting ring to it," Jordan mused as they paused in front of a door marked *Office*. "I presume there is a reason for such a handle?"

"There is. You will see." Olivia grimaced as Zeke knocked on the door.

They waited nearly a full minute before it was flung open. The man standing there made Jordan think of a large sausage stuck in a business suit. He was short of stature but oversized in the chest, and his eyes were almost completely hidden beneath a hat brim pulled low.

Brim. Aha. Clearly, the man had earned his nickname from his hat brim, which instantly tickled his suspicions. He preferred to look a man directly in his eyes when he was dealing with him.

"Come in! Come in!" Though the man's words were jovial, there was a tightness to his voice that further alarmed Jordan.

He glanced curiously around the office they were ushered into. A rickety desk canted at one angle in the center of the small room. It was piled with papers, books, ledgers, and newspapers, sticking out in every which direction. There was no secretary in sight, and the room smelled like stale cigar smoke, sweat, and something rotten. He found himself peeking at the corners of the room for a dead mouse or rat.

"I'd ask you to take a seat, but," Brim waved his large, sausage-like fingers, "as you can see, I am not set up for visitors." He shuffled his way behind his desk.

Even though you knew Zeke was visiting you today? As a precaution, Jordan positioned himself against the wall where he could see both sides of the desk. If Brim was up to no good, he'd see it coming from such a vantage point. He rested his hand on his waistcoat, within easy reaching distance of his handgun.

"What brings you to my fine establishment today, Mr. Sanford?" The man's smile was forced.

"Shipping, of course. Always shipping, sir." Zeke removed his hat and tucked it companionably beneath this arm. "We're wanting to increase our deliveries in this region from once per month to twice per month. I was hoping to determine today if your warehouses and delivery detail can handle the extra workload."

"Of course we can." Brim bellowed out a mirthless too-loud laugh that jangled Jordan's nerves. "We have the biggest warehouses on the Missouri River and the fastest crew of stage drivers in the midwest."

"Is that so?" Zeke asked mildly, raising one eyebrow. "I am glad to hear it, sir. I must confess I had my concerns, considering you are behind on your last two month's payments. Which brings me to my second order of business. You've never fallen behind before, Brim. Would it help if we set up a plan that would allow you to pay in installments?"

Brim Mulligan nodded slowly as he bent over to open his center desk drawer. In a split second, he produced a shiny silver revolver that he trained on Olivia. He moved too quickly for Jordan to do anything but draw his own pistol and train it on Brim.

"How about a new arrangement, Sanford?" the man purred in a low, rasping voice that made Jordan wonder if he was entirely sober. "One that involves forgiving our current debt and sending those new shipments our way with a thirty percent discount? Your current rates are highway robbery." With his free hand, he snatched up a handful of papers on his desk and waved them in the air.

"I've already drawn up the new contract. All it needs is your scrawl."

Jordan's blood ran hot and fast through his veins. The nerve of the man waving his weapon at an innocent lady to make a cowardly point! Brim was so intent on intimidating Sanford, Jordan wasn't certain he'd yet noticed the weapon trained on his own person.

To his credit, Zeke paled a few degrees but held his ground. He shifted uncomfortably from one foot to the next. "Now, Brim," he drawled in his habitually mild tone. "Put that gun down. I've already said we can work out an installment plan. You're very much aware Rothschild Industries already significantly undersells its competitors. We can't afford to work for free any more than you can."

"You'll not find a better deal, no matter how long and hard you look," Olivia chimed in.

To Jordan's surprise, her voice rang out a low and firm alto without the hint of a tremor. She didn't sound the least fearful of the likes of Brim nor surprised by his unconscionable behavior.

His gaze narrowed on Brim, trying to decide if he was merely bluffing or if he posed a real threat to anyone in the room. While he contemplated his next move, he noted Zeke taking a sly step closer to Olivia, putting his medium-sized frame half in front of hers — at which point, Brim shifted his muzzle an inch to the left, training it squarely on Zeke.

Yes, indeed. The man was a threat.

Though it was risky, Jordan took aim and fired, nicking the top of the man's shooting hand.

With a howl of rage and pain, Brim fell to his knees, clutching his injured hand. Thankfully, his handgun did not go off and slid harmlessly to the floor with a metallic clatter.

Jordan swiftly closed the narrow space between them and kicked the offending weapon out of reach. Keeping his own pistol trained on the fellow, he commanded harshly, "Take off your shirt." This close to the man, he was finally able to determine the source of the rotten smell. He reeked of old whiskey and vomit. "Now!" He waved his pistol like he meant business.

Brim tore at his shirt buttons, sending several of them flying. In the end, he ripped the hapless garment off, leaving nothing but the long sleeves covering his paunchy arms.

"Wrap your hand," Jordan ordered. "Tightly, so you don't bleed out. We'll notify the station master you need a physician sent your way." He curled his lip at the discarded contract on the man's desk. "As for your offer of a new deal? We cordially decline. All current agreements are null and void. No future shipments will be forthcoming."

Brim's bulbous face turned a mottled red. "You can't do that!" he roared. "It'll put me out of business." He whipped his head in Zeke's direction like a mangy dog. "Who is this man? Tell him he can't do this. He has no right!"

To Jordan's consternation, Olivia once more stepped into the fray. Her soft, warm hand settled on his wrist. "This man is my newest associate. Take a long, hard look at his face, because there is a good chance you'll be seeing him again if we don't receive those tardy payments of yours."

"I beg your forgiveness, Miss Rothschild. I can get the payments to you by the end of the week. I give you my word."

"At which time," she continued smoothly, "we will consider reinstating our original agreement and not a moment sooner. No guarantees, of course," she added sweetly. "In the meantime, we will be reevaluating our options across the region after today's display of…" She waved her hand at him in disgust. "This." There was a world of recrimination in her tone.

His head bobbed up and down like a loping jackrabbit. "I

thank you, Miss Rothschild, a hundred times over. You'll have those payments, you'll see." His wide mouth twisted down at the corners. "Your father and I went way back, dear lady. He knew my weakness for the bottle, and he understood. I am most grateful to find you are as charitable and forgiving as he." He sounded close to tears and a mite more sober than he had minutes earlier.

Olivia nodded and dug in her reticule. She came up with a few dollar bills and plopped them down on his desk. "For your doctor bill. Sometimes my new associate can be a little...intense."

"May the good Lord bless you again and again, Miss Rothschild."

Having heard enough of the man's blubbering, Jordan steered Olivia from the room. Zeke followed them outside, breathing hard as if he'd just run a long way.

"That was a close shave back there," he babbled in a voice that shook. "I am mighty grateful you asked to come along with us today, Jordan. Otherwise, things might not have turned out so well."

Jordan nodded, still too shook up over what had occurred to be in a conversational mood. He glanced down at Olivia, who was still clinging to his arm, to ensure himself again that she was safe. Now that the crisis was past, his insides were all aquiver with fear over what might have happened if he'd not been by her side with his trusty firearm.

She beamed a glorious smile up at him. There was an extra bounce in her step that made her rosy skirts swish entrancingly against his trousers. "We make capital partners, do we not? Perhaps, you might reconsider your interest in shipping, dear sir. Why, with you by my side, we would be unstoppable!" she declared dramatically.

Once back on the train, Zeke disappeared into the men's car, but Jordan lingered with Olivia just inside the doorway to her car. He nodded at Inga who gaped at them curiously from the kitchenette. "If you would give us a moment alone, Inga? This won't take long, I assure you."

"Yes, Mr. Jordan. Of course, Mr. Jordan." She bobbed a curtsy and shuffled her ample curves obediently in the direction of her tiny chamber in the rear of the car.

"What is it?" Olivia inquired breathlessly.

He pivoted to face her, keeping her hand tucked securely on his arm. "As it turns out, there is another matter of urgency I need for you to clear up for me. Right here and now."

"Yes?" Her blue eyes widened as they fixed themselves in puzzlement on his face. "Anything for my gallant savior," she added lightly.

"Are your affections engaged with Zeke Sanford?"

Her lips parted. "My what?" She blinked a few times. "With Zeke? Surely you jest!"

That was all he needed to hear. He hauled her into his arms and sealed his mouth over hers.

CHAPTER 6: HEADSTONE LADIES

OLIVIA

*O*livia threw caution to the wind beneath Jordan's onslaught of her senses and entwined her arms around his neck.

His kiss was everything she imagined it would be and more — far more. His lips were warm and cherishing, and there was an urgency to his touch that both excited and thrilled her.

"When that thug had his gun trained on you back there," he muttered against her mouth, "I died a thousand deaths."

She brushed her lips dreamily against his, making him catch his breath. "You were right," she declared softly. "About everything."

He wrapped his arms more tightly around her and buried his face against her neck. "Perhaps you might elaborate, minx?"

She shivered in delight at his endearing insult. "I can't even recall his face with any clarity," she whispered. "All I can think about is you. Just like you promised when I finally kissed the right man."

He raised his head to gaze deeply into her eyes. "Is that

what you truly think, my precious girl? That I am the right man for you?"

My precious girl. She almost swooned at his words and was grateful he was still clutching her so tightly. "I do." She reached up to touch her fingertips to his cheek, awed at what she read in his gaze. Admiration, wild concern, and a hint of vulnerability she'd never witnessed in him before. Until this very moment, he'd been all-confident and completely composed — at times, the debonair matchmaker, and at other times, the dry-humored man she was coming to adore so fiercely. "Very much so, Jordan. Go ahead. Call me impulsive and outrageous like everyone else does, but it won't change how I feel about you."

"Perhaps I'm the one who is outrageous," he groaned. "How am I going to explain this to my brother? You and I have known each other less than a week, and I am supposed to be finding you a proper husband. I'm contractually bound."

"Methinks you've succeeded in that endeavor, dear sir." She smiled mischievously at him and leaned in to brush her lips against his jaw. "I've certainly no objections to your choice of matches for me."

He chuckled ruefully but did not loosen his embrace. "I do not know the first thing about running a shipping business, darling. Nor have I any experience in managing fortunes. Make no mistake. Colt and I run a profitable business, but we are by no means wealthy. It is only right and fair to confess I do not possess the qualifications I would normally be searching for in a match for you."

"Pshaw!" She rolled her eyes at him. "We have Zeke for all that. He is trustworthy and loyal to me, and I suspect he's already taken a liking to you."

"Then it is settled?" Jordan's expression lit with cautious hope. "We have an understanding, you and I?"

"We do." She smiled. "I say, let us be outrageous together."

Her words earned her another lingering kiss that left them both short of breath.

BY THE TIME they disembarked in Headstone, Arizona a few days later, her staff was very much aware of the romance brewing between her and Jordan. That included Zeke, who, for some reason, was still traveling with them though she was fairly certain his leg of the trip was supposed to have ended in Oklahoma.

"He is so handsome, Miss Olivia, and brave and kind-hearted," Inga breathed in her ear as they stood together watching the men in their party assist with the unloading of her mountain of belongings. "I always hoped and prayed you would find a worthy husband. Your parents would be so proud."

Olivia batted damp lashes. "I believe they would be," she choked. "I am so happy, Inga! He makes me so very happy!"

"And it shows, Miss Olivia." Her maid reached over to squeeze her gloved hand. "Love looks beautiful on you, my sweet mistress."

"Love," she repeated in wonder. *Love?* Yes, it was true. The intensity of her emotions could only be described as such. She loved Jordan Branson. No, it was more than that. She was in love with him. Thoroughly and irrevocably. So much so that it made her heart tremble. Her gaze sought and found his across the crowded train platform.

He nodded at her and caressed her with his dark eyes for a moment before returning to the task at hand.

"My lands!" Inga waved her plump fingers at her face. "If any man ever looked at me that way, I would surely melt into a puddle on the ground."

Olivia cast a sideways glance at her beloved maid. "As much as it would break my heart to lose you, someday a man will look at you that way. Then he will sweep you off your feet and take you away from me," she lamented.

"Bah!" Inga waved a hand in dismissal. "There will be no sweeping this girl off her feet. Marceau stuffs me with too many of his pastries and sweetmeats. Mercy, but he is forever insisting I try this and taste that."

"Then maybe the two of you will simply have to make a match of it someday," Olivia teased. "I would not object. That way I could keep both of you in my life forever."

Inga's cheeks turned pink as the tall, dark-haired Frenchman in question glanced their way. The mild sneer he usually wore was intact, though it seemed to Olivia his gaze lingered on Inga a bit longer than necessary.

"You'll not be losing me, Miss Olivia. Not ever." Her maid gave a short titter. "As for Marceau, no one besides you and me would ever put up with all his nonsense. Therefore, I do not see you losing him, either. Mind you," her voice sharpened, "that does not mean I intend to marry the man."

The two women shared a grin as Milo bounded up to them, a travel bag in each hand. "Where to next, my lady?" He gave an exaggerated bow to his mistress while nodding cheerfully at Inga. "We await your orders."

She chuckled. "It is my understanding Zeke has arranged for us to rent a townhouse on Main Street, wherever that may be. As soon as the wagons arrive to transport our belongings, we can be on our way." Zeke was another person she planned to keep in her life as long as the Lord allowed. She could not fathom how she would get on without him. He managed her affairs so perfectly.

She'd often wondered why he remained unattached? Had he made a deathbed promise to her father to always look out for her? Or had his heart been broken previously? Or, perhaps, he had someone special in his life, after all, but was simply skilled at keeping her hidden from the rest of them. He'd always been a very private man. Private or not, she intended to have a tête-à-tête with him before his departure about her vision for the future of Rothschild Industries — a vision that included both him and Jordan.

In minutes, the vehicles in question rolled into view. She and Inga watched as the depot's cargo crew assisted in the reloading of her belongings. Before she knew it, Jordan was lifting her into the first carriage in line. He swung in after her and swooped in for a satisfying kiss as he took his seat.

She fisted her hands on his lapels. "Brazen!" she hissed. "Kissing me like that in broad daylight. What if someone sees us? Such as your brother, upon whom I would very much like to make a good impression."

"It was your idea, minx." With one last hard kiss, he settled back in his seat. "I seem to recall you insisting rather vehemently that we be outrageous together."

"A slip of the tongue you apparently do not intend to let me forget," she mused, staring out the window as their carriage began to roll.

"Not until the end of our days, precious." He reached across the seat to lace his fingers through hers. "How do you like the wild west so far, my darling debutante from the east?"

"It's different," she admitted, unsure how to put her feelings into words.

"Different in a good way or a bad way?"

"It's dustier than Boston." She was amazed the streets were composed of nothing more than hard-packed earth. Where were the cobblestones? The surrounding canyons and mesas certainly seemed rocky enough. "Does it rain much here?"

"Not nearly enough, though we do get a sand storm, now and then, being this close to the desert."

"A sand storm!" She whirled to face him. "As in a storm that rains nothing but sand?"

"Precisely. Big, heaping swirls of it," he replied grimly. "The desert can be a treacherous beast, my dear." He scooted closer to her, tucking her snugly against his side. "Fear not. I will be here to protect you." He nuzzled the curl dancing against her cheek.

"Jordan!" She spoiled the reprimand with a laugh. "You do realize we're sitting right in front of an open carriage window? Anybody walking past might see what you're about."

He reached around her to yank the curtain ties and pull them shut. "You were saying, my lady?" With one long finger, he tipped her face up to his.

"I was about to call you a cad," she confessed with a giggle. Instead, she looped her arms around his neck and tugged his head down to hers.

They arrived at her newly rented townhome far sooner than she wished. She would have preferred to remain tucked securely in Jordan's embrace until the end of time.

"I love you," he whispered huskily as their carriage rolled to a stop. "Forgive me if it is too soon to say such things, but it is true. I would give you the moon if you asked it of me." He cupped her face between his hands. "The whole world." His expression was utterly besotted.

She gazed back with her heart in her eyes. "I do not wish for the moon. Only you," she assured with a catch in her voice. "And word of your sister's whereabouts, of course," she added, touching his cheek. "Falling in love with you has only strengthened my resolve to find her."

"Is it true, Olivia?" He searched her features anxiously. "The part about loving me in return?"

She made a face at him. "Why, Mr. Branson! Do you think I go around kissing every handsome bachelor in this manner?"

He raised his brows at her.

"Don't say it!" she threatened.

"I won't say his name aloud, but have you already forgotten a certain young man back east who was not the marquis he pretended to be?"

She innocently batted her eyelashes at him. "Who? I declare I have no idea what you are yammering on about."

He chuckled and leaned in to rest his forehead against hers. "Just when I thought I couldn't adore you more..."

A gentle knock sounded on their carriage door. "Miss Olivia?" Inga's voice rang out. "We have arrived."

Olivia turned her face aside. "I am coming, Inga. One minute."

"One last kiss to fortify me?" Jordan begged softly.

Unable to resist the pleading in his voice, she took the entire minute she'd stated to her maid before opening their carriage door.

JORDAN LEAPED down and turned to assist her. She paused in the door opening. "Jordan," she intoned in a strange voice. "I do believe there is a woman in trousers on my new front porch."

He glanced over his shoulder and chuckled. "Ah, yes. That would be Hannah Donovan, the first mail-order bride we placed in Headstone. I hope you don't mind, but I sent her a telegram about our secret mission concerning my sister. That way she would be prepared to work alongside you and provide whatever resources you require." He turned back to her and winked. "The longer it takes for my brother to get the wind of it, the better. Much obliged."

"How marvelous!" So this was the notorious Hot-Tempered Hannah he'd told her about on the train ride to Headstone. The moment her toes touched the ground, she was moving in the fiery red-head's direction.

"Get the wind of what?" Colt Branson sauntered around the side of the carriage and enveloped him in a bear hug. "And what in tarnation are you doing away from our Boston office? When I received your telegram saying you were on your way, I feared all sundry of calamities had befallen you."

"Nary a one," Jordan assured, that is, if one didn't count his confrontation with the tipsy shyster, Brim Milligan. "I left our Boston office in the capable hands of Ms. Carter for a few days, so I could personally escort Miss Rothschild to Arizona." He nodded in the direction of Olivia and Hannah, who were conversing animatedly on the porch stairs. From a distance, one might have supposed they were old friends. "Alas, like our dear Meg, Olivia Rothschild is an heiress. A very wealthy one."

"More shipping money, eh?" Colt raised one brow and nodded knowingly. Olivia would make the third mail-order shipping heiress they'd helped place in a good marriage, including Callie Barra and Meg Nicholson. "It does beat all how so many fashionable young dandies back east consider marrying into a shipping family to be beneath their blue-blood standards. As if the funds and therefore the bride is somehow tainted by the means in which it was acquired. Ah, well." He clasped his hands in satisfaction. "Their sore loss is the west's great gain. Who do you have in mind for her, Jord? Will either of the grooms we have on our current waiting list be a good match?"

"Not exactly," Jordan muttered, glancing away from his brother's piercing, inquisitive gaze.

"Well, why not? Have you at least attempted to introduce her to one of them via the mail?"

"I have not. Olivia is a special case," he confessed. Here came the hard part that his older brother and business partner wasn't going to like. "As it happens, she wasn't willing to sign our standard contract after nearly being forced into marrying someone else against her will. We had to first negotiate a few amendments."

"Olivia, eh?" Colt snorted. "Already on a first-name basis, I see." He curled his upper lip. "What sort of amendments?"

Jordan shoved his hands in his pockets. *In for a penny...* There was no use beating around the bush. Best that Colt heard the truth from him, as hard as it would be to listen to it. "I reckon none of that matters any more now that she is my affianced."

Colt yanked off his Stetson. "She's your *what?*" He stomped closer, bringing them nose-to-nose. "Have you lost your ever-loving mind, brother? Have you forgotten why we started this business in the first place?"

Jordan gave him a none-too-gentle shove to create a few inches of breathing space between them. "As a matter of fact, I have *not!*" His own ire rose. "If you would just listen instead of jumping to conclusions..."

But Colt wasn't near ready to listen. "I put my entire life on hold for our mission, in case you've forgotten," he raged. "I've lived on the road, recruiting Gallant Rescuers. I've risked life and limb and kept my ear bent to the ground day and night for any word of MaryAnne's whereabouts. I've scavenged the desert and mountains, alike. And all the while you were back in Boston, doing what? Building yourself a cozy little nest in which to move on with your life! Is that the real reason for your visit?" He clenched his jaw. "You came all this way just to let me know you're abandoning me and our cause?"

Jordan hated the betrayal rolling off his brother in waves. He'd imagined their current discussion would be a difficult one, but he'd not anticipated just how difficult.

"If I might interject a moment here, gentlemen." Olivia's soft, firm voice cut through the tension in the air like a knife working its way through a gelatin. "I believe we have a lead on your sister's location at long last." The tempered excitement in her voice made both brothers' heads whip in her direction.

All Colt could do was gape at her for several seconds. "What do you know about our missing sister?" Without waiting for her response, his dark head swung in his brother's direction. "You didn't, Jordan. Please assure me you did not drag your affianced into our personal affairs. We vowed not to endanger another female in our search for MaryAnne. You promised!"

"There's been a sighting of a young woman fitting Mary-Anne's description," Olivia continued calmly as if she hadn't heard Colt's latest outburst. "Long, dark hair. Brown eyes. Not much taller than me. A tiny mole just above her upper lip on the left side."

"Where?" both brothers demanded in unison. In that moment, Jordan couldn't have been prouder of the lovely Bostonian debutante who'd captured his heart. There was so much more to her than her cultured northern accent and expensive gowns. In five minutes, she'd done what he and Colt had failed to do in five years.

"High up in the mountains, about twenty miles north of here, there's a ghost town called Rose de la Montaña."

"I've heard of it, and I've been there." Colt's voice was clipped and dismissive. "It's abandoned. That's why they call it a ghost town."

"Not any longer," Hannah Donovan cut in. Her hands were perched akimbo on her narrow hips. "Why, if you'd bothered to let me know you were still searching for your sister — and what's more, given me a proper description of her, I'd've been able to share the news with you days ago. Men!" She curled her nose in disgust. "You presume all we women do is sit around gossiping over our tea and knitting, never imagining we might be of some real use to you. Bah!" She waved both her hands at him. "Gabe knows, and he's working with Shad Nicholson and Sheriff Otera as we stand here gabbing to assemble a posse to look into the matter. I'm fairly certain the Barra brothers are in on it, too." She shook her head, grinning. "If there's any trouble afoot, you can always count on the Barras to be attracted to it like bees to honey."

OLIVIA QUICKLY PROCESSED the list of names spewing from Hannah's lips. Gabe was her husband, and Shad Nicholson was Meg's husband, a federal marshal. The Barra brothers, on the other hand, had started off as claim jumpers in town, but the three oldest had settled down with wives, compliments of Colt and Jordan's mail-order bride agency. Not only were they all living as law-abiding citizens these days, the oldest three brothers were additionally sworn in as Gallant Rescuers.

What was more, Jordan had confided in her on their train ride to Arizona, that Colt had recently and secretly sworn in both Shad Nicholson and Sheriff Otera as members of their Gallant Rescuers.

"Take me with you," she declared without preamble. She laid a hand on Jordan's arm and lifted her chin to face his older brother.

Colt was already shaking his head.

"I am the one who identified your sister and brought

word to you of the rescue posse forming up. I also have extensive contacts throughout the region due to my family's shipping business. I can help if you will let me," she reiterated coolly, holding his gaze. "She will be my family, too, when I marry your brother," she added in a gentler voice.

Colt gritted his teeth and shot another harried look at Jordon.

He merely shrugged. "A few days ago, Olivia completed a difficult business transaction while staring down the barrel of a gun. She's made of sterner stuff than she appears." He slid his arm around her waist and tugged her against his side. "We make an excellent team."

Colt scrubbed a hand over his face and clapped his Stetson back on his head, hiding the storm in his gaze. "She rides with the two of us," he grated out. "She will be under our protection at all times. Any sign of danger to her, and we retreat. That is my final offer, brother."

"I accept." Jordan gazed adoringly down at Olivia, squeezing her shoulders in a brief hug. "*We* accept."

CHAPTER 7: GHOST TOWN RENDEVOUS

OLIVIA

There wasn't much time for Olivia to move into her new townhome and unpack before she needed to be on the road again, this time on the back of a horse. Fortunately, she had Inga, Marceau, and Milo to assist her. Her chef and his younger brother hauled her parents' grandfather clock inside the entry foyer, replaced the gongs, and set it to working again.

Though smaller than the mansion where she'd grown up in Boston, Olivia's rented townhome boasted two levels. On the main level was a parlor, drawing room, dining area, and a room she instantly decided would serve as the music room and library. In the back of the home was the kitchen, storage rooms, and a small greenhouse. All the sleeping chambers were upstairs from the grand master suite, to the three guest rooms, to the servants' quarters. Olivia's room had its own powder room, but there was a second powder room down the hall that served the other rooms.

Inga busied herself unpacking her mistress's gowns, jewelry, and bed linens. Thankfully, the rental home was partially furnished with beds and armoires. They would need to purchase more furniture in the coming weeks to make the place truly comfortable.

At Colt's insistence, she and Jordan agreed to get a good night's sleep before the three of them ventured across the desert. Jordan and Zeke opted to take rooms at a boarding house on Main that Hannah Donovan recommended. It was called the Pelican's Roost.

"I'll return at daybreak with horses," Jordan promised. He raised Olivia's hand to his lips and brushed his warm mouth over her fingers. "Please assure me you packed a riding habit.

"I did." She'd packed several of them

"Good. Be sure to dress warm, precious. A coat, boots, gloves, and a hat — a real one that'll keep your head warm, not that confounded contraption dripping with peacock feathers."

She pretended to look affronted, pressing a hand to her heart. "My poor hat. And all this time, I fancied myself so sporting while wearing it."

"You would be beautiful in a flour sack, darling. Tomorrow, however, I am only concerned with utility and comfort, not appearances."

She lowered her hand. "You say such nice things sometimes, Mr. Branson. I suppose that means I'll have to forgive the slight to my feathered hat."

"Please do." He kissed her with his eyes and bid her adieu.

A knock sounded on the front door so soon after his departure that Olivia presumed he'd returned for a final word or to collect something he'd forgotten. She flung the front door wide with a teasing declaration on her lips and stopped short.

Hannah Donovan was standing there. This time, she had a beautiful red-haired infant on one hip and the other arm curled around a pile of garments.

"Dear me! What is this?" Olivia hurried to relieve the petite woman of her extra burden.

"Trousers and other warm clothing." The woman's blue-green eyes snapped with excitement and amusement. "Your menfolk might fuss about the trousers, at first, but you'll be thanking me to high heaven after a few hours on horseback."

"I'll thank you right now." Olivia laid the pile of clothing on a chair in the foyer and picked up the trousers. She held them high and wrinkled her nose critically at them. They were a herringbone weave made of brown, black, and white wool threads. "I'll confess, I've never donned a pair of these. I've never even considered donning a pair of these. However, Jordan did say he was most concerned about utility and comfort, not appearances. I'll simply have to remind him of that if he fusses too loudly."

"That's the spirit!" Hannah bent her head to nuzzle noses with her baby boy and coo something softly against his ear.

The babe gurgled with laughter and waved his tiny hands at her.

Something elemental tugged at Olivia's heart. Here was a woman who was truly happy, trousers and all. It defied all reason that a woman who owned a diamond mine would dress so boyishly, but...

"How old is he?" she inquired, trying to quench the sheer envy in her voice.

"Little Gabe is five months," Hannah returned. She beamed a smile across the foyer. "Would you like to hold him?"

"I, er..." Olivia wasn't accustomed to being around small children, but how could she say no? He was so chubby and adorable in his pristine white playsuit. "Yes. Yes, I'd love to." She tossed her borrowed trousers on the chair and reached for the babe.

Half terrified she would do something wrong like squeeze him too tightly or hold him incorrectly, she felt awkward propping Little Gabe's warm, wiggling frame against her shoulder. However, he snuggled right in, tucking his head beneath her chin and curling his tiny fingers around her crocheted collar.

"Oh-h-h-h!" she sighed softly. It was the most wonderful feeling in the world to be holding a soft, sweet smelling baby — second perhaps only to kissing Jordan. She blushed at the thought. "I want one," she confessed in a voice barely above a whisper. "One of my own someday."

"Someday might come sooner than you think." Hannah chuckled. "I saw the way Jordan Branson was looking at you earlier. The man could barely tear his eyes off you long enough to greet an old friend, not that I can blame him. You're like a fairy princess with all that white-blonde hair and that highfalutin gown of yours."

Olivia chuckled at Hannah's colorful summation of her appearance. Her dressmaker back in Boston might not appreciate her royal blue silk creation being called highfalutin, but she could tell Hannah meant no offense. She was simply one of those brutally honest creatures. "You are very kind," she murmured, rocking Little Gabe against her shoulder. She discovered she wasn't the least bit in a hurry to give him back to his mama.

"I reckon you're one of the Bransons' mail-order brides, eh?"

Apparently, the red-headed diamond mine owner was both honest *and* brazen. Olivia chuckled. "I was until Jordan and I became affianced on the train ride here."

To her surprise, Hannah clapped her hands in delight and burst out laughing as if she'd heard the jest of the century. "Oh, that is rich! A mail-order bride capturing the heart and hand of the matchmaker, himself. I cannot wait to share the news with my husband." Her laughter settled into a wide smile. "Many happy congratulations!"

"Thank you." Olivia brushed her fingertips over Little Gabe's soft, downy head of auburn hair.

"If you ask me, it's about time one of those Branson brothers found a bit of happiness for himself. Always arranging matches for others." She shook her head. "It's about time," she repeated.

OLIVIA HAD DIFFICULTY SLEEPING. Between being in a new and unfamiliar home and knowing she was going to have to rise extra early, there just hardly seemed any point in going to sleep. She tossed and turned at least a dozen times and finally dozed off in the wee hours of the morning.

"Miss Olivia?" Inga's loud whisper jolted her awake.

"Yes, Inga?" She sat up in bed, rubbing her eyes and trying to make sense of what was happening. Her brain was too fuzzy to function for a few seconds.

"It's Mr. Jordan. He's here with the horses."

"Oh, dear! Already?" Olivia leaped out of bed, stubbed her toe on a nearby chair, and hobbled the rest of the way to the powder room. There she finished waking up by splashing water from the basin on her face. Afterwards, she donned her borrowed trousers, two layers of shirts, her warmest, most comfortable set of boots, and a thick wool coat. Not bothering to style her hair, she chose instead to plait it in a simple braid that dangled past her shoulders. Only then did she pronounce herself ready.

Jordan was holding the reins to two horses when she skipped down the porch stairs.

"A good morning to you, dearest." She carried a large sack stuffed with a variety of delicious rations from Marceau.

One thing was certain. They would not go hungry on their trip.

Jordan's horse was a red and white Missouri Foxtrotter, if she properly gauged his color and breed in the morning shadows. Hers was a much smaller horse, a sleek black mare with a sparkle in her eyes and a jitter in her step. She looked anxious to let loose and run. Olivia eyed the packs tied to her haunches.

"Bed rolls, victuals, and other supplies in the event of a sandstorm or other delay," Jordan explained, as he tucked her food sack inside one of the packs. He turned around and gave her borrowed togs an approving once-over. "I see Hannah Donovan had a thing or two to say on the topic of how to dress for our mission."

"She did." Olivia grinned. "Are you completely scandalized?"

"No more than usual," he assured, bending his head to peck her on the lips.

She made a face at him while he assisted her in mounting. "As I've previously noted, you always say the nicest things to me, Mr. Branson." She tipped her nose up haughtily. "You must have attended the same finishing school as I."

He chuckled. "No. Just a boarding school for boys. Then law school." He sobered. "Maybe someday I'll get to go back and finish what I started there."

"You will," she assured. "If it is meant to be, the Lord will make a way like He always does."

"I'd like to believe that."

"What's more, you would make a good lawyer, Jordan Branson. You're fair, honest, and pleasant. So long as no one has a gun pointed at me, that is," she amended with a grin.

Colt joined them on a tall brown gelding when they passed by the livery. He kept their pace at a walk for the first mile while he flipped open a compass and fiddled with it.

"The main posse took off at daybreak, but they headed in a northeasterly route, which the sheriff claimed would provide easier access to the mountain range."

"But you don't agree," Olivia mused, interpreting his disgruntled tone.

"No. I don't." He fiddled some more with his compass. "This way," he finally announced and nudged his horse due north. He dug his heels into his gelding's flanks, and the creature broke into a canter. Olivia and Jordan urged their horses after his. The nearly twenty-mile trek flew past quicker than she expected. In less that two hours, they reached the base of the mountains that housed the Rose de la Montaña ghost town. They tied their horses in a shaded alcove and finished the last half mile or so on foot.

Hannah's sources proved correct. Rose de la Montaña was no longer abandoned. In fact, it was bustling with so much activity, it was a wonder they weren't detected during their ride across the desert. Men moved in and out of old clapboard buildings with every weapon imaginable in hand — hatchets, knives, guns, and harpoons.

The three of them secreted themselves half inside a thicket and lay on the ground, taking turns passing a spyglass around.

"Looks like we beat the main rescue party here," Colt said quietly. "Hopefully, they are not too far behind us."

To their collective dismay, there was no sign of Mary-Anne among the thugs. They watched for a full hour, and still there was no sighting of her. Another young woman, however, was present. She was a petite blonde creature, about Olivia's size. She served the men breakfast amidst many jiving calls and blown kisses, though none of them laid a hand on her.

"Well, I'll be." Colt gave a low whistle. "If I wasn't seeing this with my own eyes, I might not believe it. I'm willing to wager this is Hunter Sherrington's gang."

"Who?" Olivia hissed. She didn't recognize the name.

"A very bad hombre," Colt explained. "He's coordinated more highway hold-ups and train robberies than you can shake a stick at. Word has it, he's worth a king's fortune these days. More than likely, he's close to retirement."

Jordan nodded. "Hopefully the marshal and sheriff will catch them by surprise and capture his gang before they have the chance to scatter."

"We should head east and intercept the marshal and his posse," Olivia suggested. "Since we arrived first and got a good look at the outlaw's camp, we can share what we know and help orient the newcomers." She wasn't the least discouraged about not laying eyes on MaryAnne just yet. Her gut told her they were in the right place. It was only a matter of time before the young woman showed herself again.

"A capital idea."

It warmed her heart that Colt seemed to finally approve of something she suggested. The men collected their weapons and packs and shimmied their way along the ground to extricate themselves from the thicket. However, Olivia lingered a minute longer with the spyglass pressed to her face.

"Show yourself, MaryAnne," she muttered beneath her breath. "We've come a long way to find you." *And your brothers would do anything to be reunited with you.*

A flicker of movement in front of the old saloon caught her eye. The double doors swung wide, and out walked MaryAnne Branson.

At long last! Waving wildly with one hand behind her back in the hopes of catching the Branson brothers' attentions, she dared not take her eyes off the miracle unfolding before her.

MaryAnne would be nigh on twenty-four years by now,

considering she was Olivia's age at the time of her capture. However, she looked much older. For one thing, she was desperately thin — too thin — as if she'd not been properly nourished in ages. One side of her jawline was puckered and scarred like she'd been caught in a fire.

You poor, poor dear. Sympathy gripped Olivia. What the woman must have suffered at the hands of her captors! Alas, some things were worse than death.

She stared in amazement as the woman swaggered forth in her denim trousers and manly coat. Twin pistols appeared in her hands, which she shot in rapid succession. A pair of flying squirrels fell from one of the trees and plopped to the ground. She blew away the smoke emitting from her spent pistols and returned them to their holsters. "Top that," she cried merrily to her comrades. They clapped, cheered, and stomped their boots at her antics.

It slowly dawned on Olivia that MaryAnne wasn't being held against her will, after all. In fact, she appeared to be in charge!

One of the thugs in MaryAnne's group loped in her direction. Reaching her, he fired his own weapons, and two more squirrels came crashing down from the trees. To celebrate, he leaned over and kissed her square on the mouth.

Olivia nearly dropped her spyglass. MaryAnne Branson was no prisoner. She was running the gang, and apparently she had a beau. She shimmied backwards as fast as she could, anxious to reach the woman's brothers and report her troubling discovery.

But before she could turn around and rise to her feet, four hands reached for her and hauled her from the thicket.

"Well, what have we here?" a man muttered. "You said you thought you heard a jackrabbit. This don' look like no jackrabbit to me."

"Take her to MaryAnne," the second man growled. "She'll know what to do with her."

Olivia opened her mouth to scream in the hopes of warning Jordan and Colt, but the first man clamped a hand over her mouth. All that came out was a warbled moan.

CHAPTER 8: MORE TROUBLE

JORDAN

*J*ordan glanced over his shoulder, amused to note Olivia was still watching the camp full of hustlers, gunslingers, and no-gooders with their spyglass. He liked that she was unafraid of their mission. What was more, she seemed to be enjoying herself.

Keeping carefully concealed in the tree line, he and Colt untied their horses and prepared to ride after the marshal and sheriff's posse. It was only a matter of Olivia finishing her gawking and rejoining them.

Two dark silhouettes emerged from the ghost town and sauntered in Olivia's direction.

Mercy! Run, darling! he urged her silently. *Run.* But of course she could not hear his frantic thoughts. "Colt," he breathed, pointing.

The two of them were forced to watch in horror while she was taken captive and marched the rest of the way across the desert clearing to the ghost town. The thugs swarmed around her.

With his hands on his pistols, Jordan lunged in her direction.

"Don't!" Colt whispered harshly. His hand came down on his brother's shoulders like a vise. "It's too late. They have her. We'd best rendezvous with the others and bring backup before we go charging in there. They should arrive any minute now."

Jordan heard what he said and knew he spoke the truth, but it didn't make it any easier to turn his back on Olivia. "I can't," he muttered, swinging helplessly back in her direction.

"You can!" Colt assured. "You must!"

They rode as if jackals were chasing them and soon caught up with the posse of Gallant Rescuers, deputies, and marshals. They swiftly filled them in on the details about Olivia's capture and shared what they knew about her captors. Then they turned their horses in the direction of the camp and rode as hard and as fast as they could to Olivia's rescue.

OLIVIA'S CAPTORS threw her on her knees in front of MaryAnne. "Lookee what we discovered in the woods. Haven't been able to git 'er to talk yet, but we have to assume there are others. Pretty little thing like this wouldn't be out wandering alone."

"MaryAnne?" Olivia asked. "Is it really you?"

"Shut up!" One of her captors nudged her none too gently with the toe of his boot.

"What did you call me?" MaryAnne surveyed her dispassionately. "Never mind. Tie her to the tree." She nodded at her men. "I'll deal with her more in a bit."

Olivia's mouth fell open, but she clamped her lips shut. "You don't have to do this," she cried. "Jordan and Colt are on their way."

The woman didn't so much as flicker an eyelash. "You

must have me confused with someone else, which is neither here nor there. Regrettably, you won't be around much longer to worry your pretty little head over it."

Her accomplices chuckled with glee. "I can think of a few ways to have a little fun with this filly before Sherrington gives her the—" One of the men made a cutting motion against his neck and pretended to gag.

The other man laughed as if it was the funniest thing he'd ever heard. He swiftly tied Olivia to the trunk of an oak tree.

"No. Leave her alone for now," MaryAnne ordered. "You know the boss man has his own way of handling things."

Olivia shivered. Did that mean Hunter Sherrington would torture her? "You'll not get away with this," she sputtered fiercely. "Others are coming."

"I said shut up!"

She received another vicious kick, this time on the side of her leg. It rendered her speechless for several mind-numbing seconds.

A rumble of hooves sounded in the distance.

"I told you so," she muttered to no one in particular.

MaryAnne faced her men in alarm. "Mount up!" she bawled. She whipped a pistol from her holster and trained it on Olivia. "I'm sorry, little dove. We've not the time to deal with you any longer." With that, she took aim and fired.

Olivia never felt the bullet, but her eyesight went black and she felt her consciousness ooze away.

SHE AWOKE to the sensation of strong familiar arms surrounding her. "Jordan," she breathed. "It's you." It was a miracle, considering she'd been shot. "Am I dead or alive?"

"Very much alive, darling. You've come back to me." He hitched her closer to press his lips to her temple.

"I was shot." *Your sister shot me.*

"Where?" Jordan drew his horse to an abrupt halt.

Olivia flexed her arms and shoulders. "I feel fine." It was true, strangely true. There was not a thing wrong with her. No blood. No wounds. "How odd! I distinctly recall being shot."

Jordan nudged his horse into motion once again. "Maybe he missed."

"She," she muttered feverishly. "It was a she." *Your sister.*

She gradually became aware they were riding on horseback. "Where are you taking me?" she cried anxiously. What about MaryAnne's rescue?

"Home, precious."

"No, it's too soon. We have to go back, Jordan. I found her. I found your sister!"

"That you did, love." He hugged her more tightly. "And I thank you from the bottom of my heart."

"I'm sorry it turned out this way." Her heart clenched with sympathy for him. "I'm sorry she turned out to be one of them."

"What are you talking about, darling?"

Olivia slid her arms around his middle and laid her head against his shoulder. "MaryAnne. She wasn't a captive after all. She was leading the gang. She is the one who shot me, sweetheart."

"Hmm…" Jordan sounded puzzled. "I think I am beginning to see what happened. She must have only pretended to shoot you."

"Pretended! Whatever for?"

"She was working undercover, precious. Claims she was rescued months ago by a group of marshals who subsequently drafted her into their service. They let her go back to the gang, this time with an accomplice in tow, a fellow marshal. They've been grooming the case against

Sherrington, gathering intelligence and preparing for his arrest."

Undercover. The very notion had a romantic ring to it that tickled her senses. "Unbelievable," she muttered. "I am so happy you found your sister."

"Technically, you did the finding," he reminded.

IN A FEW HOURS, they were back in Headstone with over two dozen prisoners, some in handcuffs, some with rope tying their wrists. They filled the jail and spilled out onto the street beneath the watchful eye of the lawmen gathered.

"This is so marvelous!" Olivia cried, straightening on the horse of her affianced as they spotted the sheriff's armed deputies surrounding those who'd been captured. She squinted but could not see MaryAnne Branson among them.

A wickedly handsome man broke ranks from the crowd of arrests being made to ride their way. He doffed his hat, revealing sleek blue-black hair and a devilish grin. "Tennyson Barra, at your service, ma'am. I'm honored to meet a real live hero like yourself. May I be the first to congratulate you on assisting in the capture of one of the most notorious gangs in the west."

She flushed. "I did very little, to be truthful, other than get captured myself."

Tennyson nudged his horse abreast of them and reached out to clasp Jordan's hand. "It is good to see you again, as well. I hear other congratulation are in order?" His eyes twinkled merrily at them.

"They are," Jordan affirmed proudly. "This is Olivia Rothschild, the outrageous minx from the east who has stolen my heart."

She blushed, wishing she wasn't so dusty, disheveled, and

clad in a pair of men's trousers. She could not wait to return to her newly rented townhome to bathe and change. Next time she met one of the town citizens, she hoped to be properly dressed.

Tennyson held his gloved hand out to her. "Pleased to meet you, ma'am. It's about time someone lassoed in one of these here matchmakers. I can't tell you how good it does me to know this fellow tripped and fell into one of his own traps."

She shook hands with him, while the two men grinned at each other.

"Did we capture their leader, Hunter Sherrington?" she inquired anxiously. *And where is MaryAnne Branson? How is she faring?*

His grin slipped. "Most regrettably, we did not. He alone was missing during the raid. I fear he got away."

Disappointment clogged her throat. Did that mean her own capture had spoiled the raid MaryAnne had so painstakingly worked towards? "Oh, dear! MaryAnne must be furious with me."

"She is not. I assure you." Jordan tucked a loose strand of hair behind her ear. "Because we did manage to capture Sherrington's sister. A sassy little thing the other men have been calling Jane Sharp-Shooter Sherrington during their interrogations. She's been serving as their cook. So far, we've been unable to get a word out of her. Just sits there in her jail cell staring at the wall and looking as if the world is about to come to an end. According to MaryAnne, she's the only person left in the world Hunter cares about. She vows he will come back for her, and we'll be ready when he does."

Ah. So they still had a solid lead on the most notorious criminal in the west, one that would likely lead to his arrest. Olivia's spirits lifted. "Thank goodness," she sighed, though her heart twisted in sympathy for the poor little cook languishing in her cell. Criminal or not, her heart must be breaking at the knowledge that her capture would lead to the inevitable and subsequent arrest of her brother. She inwardly vowed to go meet the young woman at the first opportunity that presented itself. Perhaps, the sister would be willing to talk to her, another woman. It was worth a try.

"I've another bit of news to break to you," Tennyson Barra announced with a grimace. "And it's nothing good. Apparently, we had a new feller arrive into town while we were away hunting bad hombres. Says he's from Boston."

Olivia's gut twisted with foreboding. "Alec Grenville has arrived," she declared dully.

"Yes. That's the name he gave, and he's looking for you, Miss Rothschild."

"Olivia," she corrected mechanically.

"Claims he's got a legal contract for your hand in marriage, signed by your guardian. He's accompanied by his attorney, a Mr. Pickering."

"Ugh!" she muttered. "He's just happens to be the shadiest legal council in Boston."

Tennyson nodded. "I feared as much when Colt set me straight on what's going on. At any rate, I wanted to let you know we've got my oldest brother's wife, Felicity, taking a look at the documents. She's a lawyer," he explained proudly. "Already informed Mr. Pickering as well as Judge Spolidora here in town that she'll be representing you."

"I am so grateful," she murmured. This was it, the moment they'd all been dreading. The time when Zeke Sanford's trusteeship and her claim on her father's business and financial holdings would come under fire and be tested. *Let them hold, please God. Let them hold,* she begged silently.

"What I don't understand is what that fool youngest brother of mine is up to," Tennyson grumbled. "Dodge is but sixteen and all too impressionable. He's been shadowing the newcomer like he's a god, hanging on his every word, playing cards with him, introducing him to the locals, and otherwise having a jolly good time with the enemy. I apologize on behalf of the little scoundrel. Be assured he will be dealt with as soon as we finish processing the arrests of the Sherrington gang."

Olivia didn't care one whit for the notion of having the kind Tennyson Barra's youngest brother getting caught up with the likes of Alec Grenville. "You might not want to wait," she warned. "The Grenvilles are trouble. If they can find a way to use Dodge in their defense, they won't hesitate."

"Perhaps you're right. No, of course you are. I'll go have a word with him now." Tennyson made a growling sound in the back of his throat and wheeled his horse around. Before he could dig in his heels, however, a thunderous pounding of hooves sounded, and a gilded carriage came careering up Main Street. It flew past the sheriff's office and headed directly for them!

A masked man leaned out the window and trained a pistol on them.

Tennyson and Jordan danced their horses to the side of the street, tucking them protectively behind the hitching post of the General Store.

"Get behind us," Jordan growled in Olivia's ear. He set her down from his horse and frantically waved her back. He and Tennyson faced the oncoming bandit, hunkered low behind the necks of their horses, pistols at the ready.

Olivia watched in fascinated horror as several deputies broke loose from the crowd in front of the jail house and sprinted after the carriage, weapons drawn.

The carriage slid to a halt in a cloud of dust, and a pair of men leaped out. Crouching low, they crept towards Jordan and Tennyson.

"Hand over the girl," the slender one growled. It was

impossible to see his face, because of the dark strip of fabric tied over his mouth and nose, but Olivia recognized his voice. It was that of Alec Grenville. "She belongs to me. Hand her over to us now, or we're prepared to shoot."

"I can see that," Jordan replied dryly. "Perhaps we can discuss this like gentlemen over a pot of tea?"

The deputies circled the wagon and glided up behind the two would-be kidnappers on the toes of their boots.

"What do you take me for?" Alec snarled. "A complete fool?"

"As a matter-of-fact..." Jordan gave a muffled guffaw as the deputies made their move. With lightning speed and well-coordinated movements, they converged on the two rogues and brought them crashing to the ground. It happened so quickly, neither Alec nor his accomplice was able to get off a single shot.

"Well, I'll be!" Tennyson Barra lifted his Stetson to dash a bead of sweat from his forehead. "Never a dull moment around here, that's for sure."

Jordan shook his head. "All the same, we appreciate you hanging back with us here and lending your protection." He slid down from his horse and reached for Olivia.

She gladly walked into his arms. "Does this mean it's finally over?" Her voice shook, and she felt close to swooning. Her nerves were threadbare after her earlier capture, followed by her near second capture. This was more excitement than she'd ever bargained for. The west was turning out to be a wild and savage place, indeed.

Jordan snorted. "Grenville will certainly have a more difficult time enforcing a marriage contract from behind bars. A dubious contract to begin with."

"Where he'll be for a good while," Tennyson assured. "Why, the little scamp!" he exclaimed.

At his sudden change in tone and demeanor, Jordan

swiveled with Olivia in his arms to see what was amiss.

A younger version of himself was swaggering across the street in their direction.

"That is Dodge Barra," Jordan murmured in her ear.

The youngest Barra was a few inches shorter than Tennyson and boyishly thin, but there was nothing young or immature about the look of sheer male satisfaction plastered across his tanned features. He was clapping his gloved hands as if he'd just finished watching the greatest show on earth. "You did well, brother," he announced smugly. "Hunkering down like a true hero and defending the damsel in distress, but it was entirely unnecessary, I assure."

"Explain yourself, scalawag!" his older brother demanded.

"When the sheriff conducts his interrogations and examines the evidence, he will find the weapons of both Alec Grenville and his highfalutin attorney weren't even loaded. I made certain of it. Just as a precaution." With a self-satisfied smirk, he opened his fist to display a handful of shotgun shells.

Tennyson whistled. "If that doesn't beat all!" he said in wonder. "Give those to me, you little scamp."

Dodge dropped them into his brother's outstretched hand. "What?" he inquired suspiciously. "You didn't think I'd truly allied myself with such a dismal sap?" He glared up at Tennyson. "Jumping bullfrogs, you did!" His upper lip curled in disgust. "I'm a Barra, for crying out loud, and it's a fine time you start treating me like one." He shoved his hands in his pockets and hunched his shoulders so forlornly that Olivia's heart went out to him. "I was just trying to do my part while the town was empty of lawmen. When I heard what Grenville was up to, I figured I'd step in and keep him busy, show him a good time, until someone with a badge could return for a proper arrest."

"It was all your idea, wasn't it?" Olivia exclaimed in

wonder. "The whole kidnapping scheme."

He shrugged and kicked at a clod of dust on the ground. "Doesn't matter now."

"It does indeed, and I am most grateful to you!" she protested. "Riding through town like that in a fancy carriage only slowed Alec Grenville down. It was a fool thing to do, and you knew it when you suggested it to him." He'd cleverly appealed to the man's pride and lack of keen wits.

Dodge's expression lit with gratitude. "Maybe," he muttered. A half-grin played at the edges of his mouth.

"And you sent him right past the sheriff's office in plain view of a half dozen deputies — *after* relieving them of their ammunition." She shook her head chuckling. It was genius of the lad, truly genius. "Tennyson Barra, I do believe your youngest brother single-handedly took down a pair of rogues without firing a shot." Her voice shook with gratitude. She disengaged herself from the arms of her affianced and flew in the lad's direction.

He stood there in wide-eyed amazement as she threw her arms around him. "You're my hero," she declared damply. "You saved me from a heap of legal shenanigans, and I shall be eternally grateful."

"Aw, ma'am." His rope-like arms came around her in a gentle hug. "It was nothing, I assure you."

"It was everything." She pulled back and held him at an arm's length. "Because of you, I am going to marry the man I love with no further interference. I will see that you are suitably rewarded. What is it that you want? A new horse? A—"

"That'll be quite enough," Tennyson interrupted. "The Barra brothers won't be taking payment for helping out a lady in trouble." He rode over to them and held out one large hand. "Hop on up, boy. I'll take you home."

Grinning from ear to ear, Dodge ignored his hand and leaped on the back of his steed unassisted.

EPILOGUE

One week later

*O*livia stood before her long oval dressing mirror in her bedchamber, hardly recognizing the woman in white staring back at her. There'd been no time to procure a wedding gown of her own, but that hadn't posed a problem to the spunky, resourceful mail-order brides of Headstone. Tennyson's wife, Callie, had lent her one so magnificent that it made her feel like a princess to have it on. Like Olivia, Callie was a shipping heiress. Lucky for her, though, her parents were still very much alive. In fact, they'd relocated from the east and built a fortress of a home in Headstone to be nearer to their daughter and future grandchildren.

"It's a perfect fit!" Callie pronounced in satisfaction. She was a red-head like Hannah and equally ravishing. She stooped in her Sunday-best lavender gown to fluff up the cascade of white lace and silk skirts around Olivia's ankles. "Why, your Inga is a veritable magician with a needle and a spool of thread." They'd had to raise the hem an inch or two to accommodate her shorter height.

"You are lovely, indeed." Meg Nicholson poked at a few pins in Olivia's hair and stood on tiptoe to tuck a white rosette against the elaborate blonde twists she'd created. She was dressed in a gown of ivory and mauve wool with a high-waist to cover the fact she'd recently delivered a babe. She and Shad were the proud parents of a wee little girl. "That's it. You're ready, my sweet friend. Jordan won't be able to think straight when he catches sight of you."

Hannah grinned mischievously at her in the mirror. She was peeking over Olivia's left shoulder. "You'll do," she assured with a decided nod. She tugged at the high neck of her emerald green gown. "I'm still debating whether or not to forgive you, though, for denying my request to wear trousers to your wedding."

The other five women in the room erupted into giggles.

Daisy Barra, who was Callie and Felicity's newest sister-in-law now that she'd married Prescott, shyly held out a necklace on a silver chain. It boasted a sparkling blue sapphire teardrop pendent that matched the sky-blue gown she was wearing. "The lace handkerchief Madge Barra lent you is something old. Your bouquet of hothouse roses is something new. Callie's wedding gown is something borrowed, but you still need something blue. This belonged to my grandmother. I'd be honored if you'd wear it. You're one of us now, you know."

One of them. Olivia surveyed the necklace in awe, awash with the thrill of being accepted by such an amazing group of lady friends. Though she was still getting to know them, she already adored each and every one of the brave and spirited mail-order brides. "It's stunning." She'd never seen a sapphire so large or luminous. "I thank you with all my heart. Will you help me put it on?"

"Yes, of course." Daisy stepped behind Olivia to secure the

clasp. It made a breathtaking addition to her wedding ensemble.

Standing across the room by the window was her new attorney, Felicity Barra, whose services had turned out to be thankfully unneeded. She was clutching Olivia's flower bouquet in her hands. "They've arrived," she reported excitedly. "The minister and his wife are stepping from their carriage as I speak. The judge is accompanying them." She spun to face the other women in a swirl of navy skirts. Her rich brunette hair was pulled back in a set of thick coils, but a few tendrils had escaped to wave entrancingly around her temples and cheeks. "It is time!"

As previously decided, they filed out of Olivia's bedchamber in the order they'd been married. Hannah headed up their entourage, followed by Callie, Felicity, Meg, and Daisy in their rainbow of gowns. Olivia glided behind them in her old, new, borrowed, and blue wedding gown, flowers, and jewelry. The women slowly descended the stairs to the small crowd awaiting them in the drawing room. A few chattering guests had spilled into the entry foyer, but they fell silent as the women approached.

A trio of stringed instruments struck the opening notes, and Olivia began her bridal march to the front of the drawing room.

Jordan awaited her at the marble mantle where the minister was stationed. He was wearing a black suit over a snowy white shirt with his heart in his eyes. His brother was standing to his right, and the husbands of the mail-order brides were extended in a long line beyond Colt, starting with Gabe Donovan, Hannah's ruggedly handsome husband. The tall, dark, and towering Tennyson and Levi Barra were next. Then there was the dashing marshal, Shad Nicholson, who was a few inches shorter than the Barras. Bringing up the end of the line was Daisy's husband, Prescott Barra. Though clad in a dark suit like the rest of the men, his jacket was unbuttoned, revealing twin pistols slung around his waist.

Olivia blinked at the weapons he was making no effort to hide, and suppressed a grateful shiver. One never knew when that sort of protection might be needed here in the oh-so-wild west, not that she could imagine anyone being so foolish as to try something on her wedding day. There were too many brave and brawny cowboys in the room for that.

She lifted her gaze to her beloved's and promptly forget about everyone and everything in the room but him.

"I love you," he mouthed silently to her.

She glided the final few steps to him in a haze of happiness. "I love you, too," she whispered when they were facing each other, hands clasped between them.

"Dearly beloved," the minister droned. "We gather here today to join this man and this woman in holy matrimony."

Emotion welled up her throat as she thought of how proud her parents would be if they could see her now. Against all odds, she'd successfully evaded her aunt's long litany of schemes for her future and found the man of her dreams, one most worthy of taking the helm of Rothschild Industries. He didn't want it, neither the money nor the power, which was what made him so perfect for the task.

They repeated their vows in awed, hushed tones, unable to tear their gazes away from each other.

"I now pronounce you man and wife, Mr. and Mrs. Jordan Branson." The minister beamed at them. "You may kiss your bride, sir."

Jordan drew her into his arms and brushed his lips adoringly against hers. "My love. My wife," he whispered huskily.

They turned to face the room full of friends, townsfolk,

and dignitaries. Judge Spolidora was present along with the mayor and several visiting federal marshals who were helping conduct the lengthy interrogations of the Sherrington gang. MaryAnne stood in the back of the drawing room, her lips forming a flat, somber line. The unmarred side of her face was canted towards the other guests, her scars carefully averted. Olivia wanted to run to her, to assure her that time and the grace of the Lord would heal every wound mirrored in her eyes. Her story was a dark and sad one that Olivia had yet to piece together in its entirety. Suffice to say, it had solidified her brothers' determination to keep their bridal agency alive and operating at full speed. They were adamant that no other young woman would suffer the way she had and were privately negotiating to bring their sister on board their business in some capacity.

Olivia's gaze drifted over the others assembled in the room, until she was able to pick out Madge's smiling features and damp eyes. She was the Barra brothers' half-sister. Unlike her striking brothers, she was a plainer, more demure creature in a simple gown of dove gray with her salt and pepper hair pulled back in a French twist. Dodge was at her side, smirking proudly as if the entire wedding was his doing. In truth, it rather was.

Breathing a prayer of gratitude and thanksgiving, Olivia allowed herself a moment to revel in amazement at how large a crowd had gathered to celebrate her union to Jordan. The outpouring of love and support for a newcomer like herself and her husband, who'd only visited the town on a few occasions, was truly impressive and heartwarming. It was as if the entire town was one big family, and no wonder. Hannah and Gabe's yellow diamond mine at Hope's Landing on the outskirts of Headstone employed over half the menfolk in town. The Barra brothers and Madge were part-owners. Plus, it seemed that most, if not all, the local lawmen were now sworn members of the Branson's Gallant Rescuers.

"Thank you," she murmured to her new husband, "for making me yours. For making me a part of all this." For the first time in years, she felt like she had a family again. Like she belonged.

Jordan's smile was tender and knowing. "We can stay in town as long as you like, darling."

"And visit as often as we please." She cuddled closer, with both hands wrapped around his strong arm. "But we are needed in Boston, dearest. Both of us. Rothschild Industries won't run itself, and you've started a good work with the Boomtown Mail Order Brides Company. Just look around and see for yourself how much happiness you've helped bring to this community. We can't stop now. We can't ever stop, Jordan."

"Because of MaryAnne," he said softly.

"And all the brides who came after her," Olivia added.

"And all those yet to come," he finished. Heedless of their sizable audience, he bent his head over hers to press another kiss to her most willing lips.

"Jordan," she hissed, trying not to giggle. "Behave your-self! There are witnesses. A great many of them this time."

"Never!" His dark eyes glowed with love and promise. "Not so long as I get to live and breathe by the side of such a lovely and outrageous little minx."

I hope you loved
OUTRAGEOUS OLIVIA!
Please leave a review.
Then turn the page for an excerpt from

Jinglebell Jane

about a young beauty with a reputation for trouble and the clever cowboy plotting her arrest.

Much love,
Jovie

SNEAK PREVIEW: JINGLEBELL JANE

*I*t was the first week of November, normally Jane Sherrington's favorite time of year. She idly traced a finger down one of the iron bars of her jail cell. What few trees, shrubs, and flowers there were in the deserts of Arizona would be shedding their leaves and blooms by now. The air would be getting brisk at night — more than likely a degree or two cooler than when she'd been captured a week earlier. Eight days, three hours, and twenty-one minutes to be precise.

She was very accurate at keeping time. If asked, she could recite to the minute how long it had been since she and her brother, Hunter, had run away from the home of their horrid uncle, who'd proven to be an equally horrid guardian. She could recount how many years, months, and weeks they had been on the road and how many trains and stagecoaches her brother and his comrades had held at gunpoint and robbed. She also knew exactly how many days her brother had been missing from their camp, high on the Rose de la Montaña, which was the only reason he'd avoided capture like herself and the rest of his gang. What she didn't know was when he would return for her. All she knew was that he would.

And the thought terrified her.

"Miss Sherrington, let us try this again, shall we?" Sheriff Chase Otera had a sigh in his voice and a sympathetic glint in his dark gaze as he pulled up a chair outside her cell. He took a seat and unfolded his list of handwritten questions she'd refused to answer thus far.

He was roughly the age her father would have been if he was still alive, and she could tell it troubled him greatly to have a woman housed in his jail. His sympathies had worked to her advantage, though. So far, his kindness had garnered her a pillow and a soft wool blanket, a fresh change of clothing, and a tiny sliver of apple pie. Alas, it had garnered her nothing in which to pick a lock or otherwise escape her confinement.

"To the best of your knowledge, Miss Sherrington, where is your brother?"

She remained standing in front of the bars separating them, but she lowered her lashes. It didn't matter how many questions he asked, her answer was the same.

I do not know.

With a grimace at her silence, the sheriff moved on to his next question. "Do you know what heist he is planning next?"

I do not know.

Jane wished she knew. Quite honestly, she couldn't state with any clarity if her brother was even still alive. It had always been like this between them. He came and went as he pleased, often being gone days or weeks at a time. Because of the number of lawmen who had him on their most wanted lists, she never knew when his next visit would be or if it would be his last. Such were the risks of living a life of crime.

Jane tried not to wince with each question as the sheriff of Headstone worked his way through his long list, bracing herself for the hardest one — the one with which he always ended his interrogations. Jane blinked back tears, because it was a topic that haunted her day and night. Forcing her eyes wide open in the attempt to control her emotions, she blindly fastened her gaze on the shiny silver badge fastened to the breast pocket of his vest. She respected what it stood for and longed more than anything to be on the other side of these iron bars...on the right side of the law. Her heart was already there. It had always been there.

"Will your brother come back for you, Miss Sherrington?"

"I do not know!" The answer wrenched itself from her before she could call it back, stunning them both with the fact she'd broken her silence at last. It was a relief for Jane to finally bear her soul to the kindhearted sheriff; however, terror clenched her insides. Terror at what her brother might do if he found out she had cooperated with the investigation. Nobody ratted anybody out in their gang. It was their number one rule in the event of capture. Nobody talked. *Ever!*

"I, er...thank you for answering the question." Sheriff Otera shifted in his seat, fiddled with his pen and paper, and appeared to be struggling to overcome his amazement. "I know this whole ordeal has been difficult for you, ma'am."

"It is," she said in a voice barely above a whisper.

"But if you will simply finish answering my questions, there is a distinct possibility I may be able to let you go free."

Free. The word made Jane's tears spring forth in a full gush. She wanted her freedom more than anything in the world, but she would never be free — not while Hunter Sherrington was on the loose.

"I do not know," she repeated in a shaky voice. "It is my only answer to every one of your questions, sir. I am telling the truth. I quite simply do not know. I never do. My brother keeps his own council."

He confided in no one, not even to MaryAnne Branson, whom he'd most unwittingly made his second-in-charge. MaryAnne, as it turned out, had been turned by a group of federal marshals during a previous capture and had returned to the gang in an undercover role for the sole purpose of assisting in the gang's arrest. Which she had done in spades. Everyone in Hunter Sherrington's gang was now behind bars, including his own sister — everyone, that is, except Hunter Sherrington, himself.

"Miss Branson said the same. Your story agrees with hers one hundred percent." Sheriff Otera stood and scrubbed a hand wearily across his jaw. It was getting late, and an evening shadow was manifesting itself across the lower half of his face. "In fact, every member of your brother's gang, whom we have in our custody, shares the same story about your involvement. Though none can offer any proof, every one of them claims you are innocent of all wrongdoing. Is that also true, Miss Sherrington?"

Am I innocent? MaryAnne made no effort to dash away the tears still trickling one over the other down her cheeks. She didn't feel innocent. She felt older than her years. Bitter. Jaded. "I know what sort of man my brother is, sheriff. I think I've always known." She understood the circumstances leading up to his decision to step outside the boundaries of the law, but she also understood that he was wrong — very wrong. She'd spent the last five of her seventeen years trying to change his mind, trying to coax him into leaving his criminal activities behind.

She averted her face from the sheriff, no longer able to

bear the concern and sympathy mirrored in his fatherly gaze. She was the sister of a notorious criminal. Nothing would ever remove that stain from her name or reputation. She could drift and she could survive, but she would never belong anywhere.

The sound of metal clanging against metal made Jane jump. "What are you doing, sir?" she gasped, whipping her face around. Unless she was dreaming or imagining things, the sheriff was unlocking her jail cell.

"Letting you go," he returned mildly. "You answered my questions, and I am a man of my word."

"But—" She raised and lowered her hands. *I have no place to go. No money. No friends.* At one point, she'd considered MaryAnne Branson to be her friend, but she was no longer so sure. The woman hadn't hesitated to rat out the entire gang and land them all in jail, making a dangerous enemy of Hunter in the process. Not to mention, MaryAnne had not once visited Jane while she was behind bars.

Hunter would exact his revenge on MaryAnne, in his own way and in his own time. It would be swift and thorough. Jane would just as soon not be caught in the crossfire when that day came.

"I imagine it will take a little time to get back on your feet, so to speak." Sheriff Otera opened her cell door wide and eyed her in concern. "Since it's getting late, I've arranged for a lovely townswoman by the name of Felicity Barra to board you for the night. She's an attorney, in the event you wish to seek legal council."

A woman who is an attorney? Jane stared at the sheriff in awe. Until this very moment, she hadn't realized it was even possible for a woman to serve as an attorney.

"Her husband, Levi, runs a ranch across town, has three younger brothers, and all of them are part-owners in the yellow diamond mind over yonder at Hope's Landing."

Diamonds? A shiver of foreboding worked its way through Jane's slender shoulders. As soon as her brother caught wind of it, another heist would be in the making. He wouldn't be able to resist helping himself to a hidden cache of diamonds. "That is very kind of you," she mumbled. "I do not know how I will ever be able to repay you." More than likely, her only "payment" would come in the form of a rabid brother who would tear his way through Headstone, exacting revenge for the capture of his sister and comrades.

"Think nothing of it." Sheriff Otera waved a hand in dismissal. "It's the least we can do to recompense you for the length of your detainment. I'll send a deputy to fetch my wagon, and I'll drive you there myself."

AS THE SHERIFF'S wagon rolled down Main Street, Jane fingered the long blonde braid trailing over her shoulder, wondering what Felicity and Levi Barra would be like. Would they be kind? Suspicious of Jane? Vengeful in attitude after all the horrible things the Sherrington gang had done?

They drove past the town square, and Jane caught her breath at the sight of the Christmas tree on display. Red ribbons draped it, and candles flickered from the outermost branches. At the very top, a metal star caught the fading sunlight and glowed a rosy gold.

"We had the tree lighting last night," Sheriff Otera offered. "Wish you could have attended it." He sounded regretful.

Jane stared at him in wonder. What kind of sheriff cared about frivolous stuff like that? Didn't he have his hands full processing all the indictments of the Sherrington gang members?

"Ah, here we are." He nosed his team of horses up a long, hard-packed earthen drive. A wide, sprawling farmhouse rose in the distance. It looked freshly whitewashed and boasted a wide, inviting front veranda. A dog barked, cows bayed, and the dying shoots of what used to be a cornfield waved dryly in the evening breezes.

A tall, slim cowboy was lounged against one of the posts at the top of the porch stairs. He pushed away from his post and straightened at their approach.

"Well, what do you know? That looks like Dodge." Sheriff Otera slowed his horses and brought them to a standstill in front of the farmhouse. "He's the youngest Barra brother, the only one that isn't married yet. He's but sixteen, maybe seventeen. Think I recall hearing something about a birthday not too long ago."

Just like me. I am seventeen. Heartbeat quickening in excitement and curiosity, Jane squinted through the twilight, trying to get a better look at the lad. She couldn't remember the last time she'd encountered someone her age. Sure, she saw them in passing in the towns her brother and his cronies were about to rob, but she'd never been allowed to engage them in any way. To learn their names. Much less hold a conversation.

She swayed in her seat, feeling suddenly off balance. What would she say to this Dodge Barra, when she had the chance? How should she act? They might as well have been raised on different planets for how little they would have in common. More than likely, he'd grown up with a roof over his head and three square meals a day, not to mention a proper education. She'd enjoyed none of those things.

The teen in question loped down the porch stairs two at a time and swaggered to her side of the carriage.

Jane stared at him with a mixture of fear and fascination and discovered no censure in his dark eyes, only curiosity and shrewd speculation.

He was dressed humbly in faded denim trousers, scuffed

boots, and a plaid shirt rolled at the sleeves. She was surprised at how tanned and muscular his arms were.

Doffing a well-worn brown Stetson, he revealed longish blue-black locks that tangled roguishly with his collar. He certainly didn't look like the owner of a diamond mine.

"Howdy there, sheriff." He shot a devilish grin across the wagon seat to her escort. "I gather this young lady is the Jinglebell Jane everyone across town has been carrying on about?"

Jinglebell Jane. She caught her breath, as wonder flooded her. No one had ever teased her like that, nor had she ever before boasted a nickname. It was so fun and unexpected...so freakishly normal!

I hope you enjoyed this excerpt from
Jinglebell Jane.

This complete 12-book series is available now in eBook, paperback, and Kindle Unlimited on Amazon.

Read them all!
Hot-Tempered Hannah
Cold-Feet Callie
Fiery Felicity
Misunderstood Meg
Dare-Devil Daisy
Outrageous Olivia
Jinglebell Jane
Absentminded Amelia
Bookish Belinda
Tenacious Trudy
Meddlesome Madge

Mismatched MaryAnne
MOB Rescue Series Box Set Books 1-4
MOB Rescue Series Box Set Books 5-8
MOB Rescue Series Box Set Books 9-12

Much love,
Jovie

GET A FREE BOOK!

Join my mailing list to be the first to know about new releases, free books, special discount prices, Bonus Content, and giveaways.

https://BookHip.com/GNVABPD

NOTE FROM JOVIE

Guess what? I have some Bonus Content for you. Read a
little more about the swoony cowboy heroes in my books by
signing up for my mailing list.
There will be a special Bonus Content chapter for each new

book I write, just for my subscribers. Plus, you get a FREE book just for signing up!

Thank you for reading and loving my books.

JOIN CUPPA JO READERS!

If you're on Facebook, you're invited to join my group, Cuppa Jo Readers. Saddle up for some fun reader games and giveaways + book chats about my sweet and swoon-worthy cowboy book heroes!

https://www.facebook.com/groups/CuppaJoReaders

SNEAK PEEK: ELIZABETH

Early November, 1866

*E*lizabeth Byrd rubbed icy hands up and down her arms beneath her threadbare navy wool cloak as she gingerly hopped down from the stagecoach. It was so much colder in northern Texas than it had been in Georgia. She gazed around her at the hard-packed earthen streets, scored by the ruts of many wagon wheels. They probably would have been soft and muddy if it weren't for the brisk winds swirling above them. Instead, they were stiff with cold and covered in a layer of frost that glinted like rosy crystals beneath the setting sun.

Plain, saltbox buildings of weathered gray planks hovered over the streets like watchful sentinels, as faded and tattered as the handful of citizens scurrying past — women in faded gingham dresses and bonnets along with a half-dozen or so men in work clothes and dusty top hats. More than likely, they were in a hurry to get home, since it was fast approaching the dinner hour. Her stomach rumbled out a contentious reminder at how long it had been since her own last meal.

So this was Cowboy Creek.

At least I'll fit in. She glanced ruefully down at her workaday brown dress and the scuffed toes of her boots. Perhaps, wearing the castoffs of her former maid, Lucy, wasn't the most brilliant idea she'd ever come up with. However, it was the only plan she'd been able to conjure up on such short notice. A young woman traveling alone couldn't be too careful these days. For her own safety, she'd wanted to attract as little attention as possible during her long journey west. It had worked. Few folks had given her more than a cursory glance the entire trip, leaving her plenty of time to silently berate herself for accepting the challenge of her dear friend, Caroline, to change her stars by becoming a mail-order bride like she and a few other friends had done the previous Christmas.

"Thanks to the war, there's nothing left for us here in Atlanta, love. You know it, and I know it," Caroline had chided gently. Then she'd leaned in to embrace her tenderly. "I know you miss him. We all do." She was referring to Elizabeth's fiancé who'd perished in battle. "But he would want you to go on and keep living. That means dusting off your broken heart and finding a man to marry while you're still young enough to have a family of your own."

She and her friends were in their early twenties, practically rusticating on the shelf in the eyes of those who'd once comprised the social elite in Atlanta. They were confirmed spinsters, yesterday's news, has-beens...

Well, only Elizabeth was now. Her friends had proven to be more adventurous than she was. They'd responded to the advert a year earlier, journeyed nearly all the way across the continent, and were now happily married.

Or so they claimed. Elizabeth was still skeptical about the

notion of agreeing to marry a man she'd never met. However, Caroline's latest letter had been full of nothing but praise about the successful matches she and their friends had made.

Be assured, dearest, that there are still scads of marriageable men lined up and waiting for you in Cowboy Creek. All you have to do is pack your bags and hop on a train. We cannot wait to see you again!

Caroline had been the one to discover this startling opportunity by reading an advert in The Western Gentlemen's Gazette. It had been placed there by a businessman who claimed to be running the fastest growing mail-order bride company in the west.

All I had to do is pack my bags and leave behind everyone and everything I've ever known to take part in the same opportunity. Elizabeth shivered and pulled her cloak more tightly around her. Attempting to duck her chin farther down inside the collar, she wondered if she'd just made the biggest mistake of her life. She was in Cowboy Creek several days later than she'd originally agreed to arrive, having wrestled like the dickens with her better judgment to make up her mind to join her friends.

Oh, how she missed the three of them! Caroline, Daphne, and Violet were former debutantes from Atlanta, like herself. All were from impoverished families whose properties and bank accounts had been devastated by the war. It was the only reason Elizabeth had been willing to even consider the foolish idea of joining them. She was fast running out of options. Her widowed mother was barely keeping food on the table for her three younger sisters.

Even so, it had been a last-minute decision, one she'd made too late to begin any correspondence with her intended groom. She didn't even know the man's name, only that he would be waiting for her in Cowboy Creek when her stagecoach rolled into town. Or so Caroline had promised.

With a sigh of resignation, Elizabeth reached down to grasp the handles of her two travel bags that the stage driver had unloaded for her. The rest of her belongings would arrive in the coming days. There'd been too many trunks to bring along by stage. In the meantime, she hoped and prayed she was doing the right thing for her loved ones. At worst, her reluctant decision to leave home meant one less mouth for Mama to feed. At best, she might claw her way back to some modicum of social significance and be in the position to help her family in some way. Some day…

Her hopes in that regard plummeted the second she laid eyes on the two men in the wagon rumbling in her direction. It was a rickety vehicle with no overhead covering. It creaked and groaned with each turn of its wheels, a problem that might have easily been solved with a squirt of oil. Then again, the heavily patched trousers of both men indicated they were as poor as church mice. More than likely, they didn't possess any extra coin for oil.

Of all the rotten luck! She bit her lower lip. *I'm about to marry a man as poor as myself.* So much for her hopes of improving her lot in life enough to send money home to Mama and the girls!

The driver slowed his team, a pair of red-brown geldings. They were much lovelier than the rattle-trap they were pulling. "Elizabeth Byrd, I presume?" he inquired in a rich baritone that was neither unpleasant nor overly warm and welcoming.

Her insides froze to a block of ice. This time, it wasn't because of the frigid temperatures of northern Texas. She recognized that face, that voice; and with them, came a flood of heart wrenching emotions.

"You!" she exclaimed. Her travel bags slid from her nerveless fingers to the ground once more. A hand flew to her heart, as she relived the sickening dread all over again that she'd experienced at the Battle of James Island. She was the unlucky nurse who'd delivered the message to Captain David Pemberton that his wife had passed during childbirth. The babe hadn't survived, either. But what, in heaven's name, was the tragic officer doing so far from home? Unless she was mistaken, his family was from the Ft. Sumpter area.

"Nurse Byrd." The captain handed his reins to the man sitting next to him, a grizzled older fellow who was dressed in a well-pressed brown suit, though both knees bore patches. "We meet again." He offered her a two-fingered salute and reached for her travel bags. He was even more handsome than she remembered, despite the well-worn Stetson shading his piercing bourbon eyes. During their last encounter, he'd been clean shaven. His light brown sideburns now traveled down to a shortly clipped beard. If the offbeat rhythm of her heart was any indication, he wore the more rugged look rather nicely.

Which was neither here nor there. Elizabeth gave herself a mental shake. She'd been searching for a sign, anything that would shed light on whether she was doing the right thing by coming to Cowboy Creek. Encountering this man, of all people, only a handful of minutes after her arrival, seemed a pretty clear indication of just how horrible a mistake she'd made.

She nudged the handles of her bags with the toe of her boot to put them out of reach. "Y-you don't have to go through with this, captain. I can only imagine how difficult it is for you to lay eyes on me again." If it was anything close to how difficult it was for her to lay eyes on him, it would behoove them both to take off running in opposite directions. "I am quite happy to board with one of my friends

JO GRAFFORD, WRITING AS & JOVIE GRACE

until I can secure passage back to Georgia." The whole trip had been a horrible miscalculation of judgment. She could see that now as she stared stonily into the face of the officer who'd led the man to whom she was once affianced into the battle that had claimed his life. Captain Pemberton didn't know that wretched fact, of course. How could he? They were neither personally, nor closely, acquainted at the time.

The expression in his eyes softened a few degrees as he regarded her. "I gather you found the young man you were searching for during the war?" he noted quietly. "Otherwise, you would not be here."

Preparing to marry you, you mean! "I found him, yes." Her voice was tight with cold and misery. It was all she could do to keep her teeth from chattering. "I found him and buried him."

"Ah." He nodded sadly. "Words are never adequate in situations like these. Nevertheless, I am deeply sorry for your loss."

His regret appeared genuine. She sensed he was a kind man, a good man, despite the deplorable circumstances under which they'd made their first acquaintance. *More's the pity!* Though she couldn't exactly hold the captain responsible for the Union bullet that had taken her Charley's life, she couldn't just up and marry the man responsible for leading him into harm's way, either. Could she?

Perhaps it was the cold breeze numbing her brain, but suddenly she was no longer certain about a good number of things.

"Come, Elizabeth." The commanding note in David Pemberton's voice brooked no further arguments. "You must be famished after such a long journey, and you'll catch your death out here if we linger in the cold."

This time, Elizabeth's toes were too icy to function when he reached for her travel bags. She stood there shivering while he tossed them inside his wagon. She was both shocked and grateful when he proceeded to unbutton his overcoat and slide it around her shoulders.

It was toasty warm from his body heat and smelled woodsy and masculine. "I th-thank y-you." She was no longer able to hide how badly her teeth were chattering.

"Think nothing of it, Miss Byrd." He slid a protective arm around her shoulders and guided her on down the street. "A friendly fellow named Frederick owns the eatery next door. Since our wedding isn't for another two hours, how about we head over there for a spell? We can grab a bite to eat and thaw out at the same time."

Our wedding? Her lips parted in protest, but she was shivering too hard to form any words.

As if sensing her confusion, he smiled and leaned closer to speak directly in her ear. His breath warmed her chilly lobe and sent a shot of…something straight down to her toes. "Surely an angel of mercy like yourself can spare the time to swap a few war stories with an old soldier?"

She clamped her teeth together. *An angel of mercy, indeed!* She'd felt more like an angel of death back there on the battlefield. There were days she lost more soldiers than the ones she managed to save. It was something she preferred never to think of again, much less discuss.

"If I cannot make you smile at least once in the next two hours, I'll purchase your passage back to Atlanta, myself," he teased, tightening his arm around her shoulders.

Now *that* was an offer she couldn't afford to pass up. She didn't currently possess the coin for a return trip, though she had to wonder if the shabbily dressed captain was any better for the funds, himself.

She gave him a tight-lipped nod and allowed him to lead her inside the eatery.

The tantalizing aromas of fresh-baked bread, hot cider,

and some other delectable entrée assailed them, making her mouth water. A pine tree graced one corner of the dining area. Its boughs were weighed down with festive gingerbread ornaments and countless strands of red ribbon. A man in a white apron, whom she could only presume was Captain Pemberton's friend, Frederick, cut between a line of tables and hurried in their direction, arms outstretched. "You rebel you! Someone might have at least warned me you were one of the lucky fellers gittin' himself a new wife."

"Oh-h!" Elizabeth's voice came out as a warble of alarm as, from the corner of her eye, she watched a young serving woman heading their way from the opposite direction. She was bearing a tray with a tall cake and holding it in such a manner that she couldn't see over the top of it. She was very much at risk of running in to someone or something.

David Pemberton glanced down at her concern, but all she could do was wave her hand in the direction of the calamity about to take place.

His gaze swiftly followed where she pointed, just in time to watch the unfortunate server and her cake collide with Frederick. White icing and peach preserves flew everywhere. His hair and one side of his face were plastered with a layer of sticky whiteness.

The woman gave a strangled shriek and slid to her knees. A puppy dashed out of nowhere and began to lick the remains of the gooey fluff from her fingers.

Afterwards, Elizabeth would blame it on the long journey for frazzling her nerves to such an extent; because, otherwise, there was no excuse on heaven or earth for what she did next.

She laughed — hysterically! It was ill-mannered of her, unladylike to the extreme, and completely uncalled for, but she couldn't help it. She laughed until there were tears in her eyes.

Captain Pemberton grinned in unholy glee at her. There was such a delicious glint in his whiskey eyes that it made her knees tremble.

"A deal's a deal, nurse; and the way I see it, you did more than smile. You laughed, which means I'll not be needing to purchase that trip back to Atlanta for you, after all. Unless you've any further objections, we've a little less than two hours before we say our vows." He arched one dark brow at her in challenge.

Their gazes clashed, and the world beneath her shifted. As a woman of her word, she suddenly couldn't come up with any more reasons — not a blessed one — why they couldn't or shouldn't get married.

Tonight!

I hope you enjoyed this excerpt from
Elizabeth
Available now on in eBook, paperback, and Kindle Unlimited on Amazon.

Read the whole trilogy!
Elizabeth
Grace
Lilly

Much love,
Jovie

ALSO BY JOVIE

For the most up-to-date printable list of my sweet historical books:

Click here

or go to:

https://www.jografford.com/joviegracebooks

For the most up-to-date printable list of my sweet contemporary books:

Click here

or go to:

https://www.JoGrafford.com/books

ABOUT JOVIE

Jovie Grace is an Amazon bestselling author of sweet and inspirational historical romance books full of faith, family, and second chances. She also writes sweet contemporary romance as Jo Grafford.

1.) Follow on Amazon!
https://www.amazon.com/stores/Jovie-Grace/author/B09SB1V58Q

2.) Join Cuppa Jo Readers!
https://www.facebook.com/groups/CuppaJoReaders

3.) Follow on Bookbub!
https://www.bookbub.com/authors/jovie-grace

4.) Follow on Facebook!
https://www.facebook.com/JovieGraceBooks

Made in United States
North Haven, CT
16 September 2024

57445893R00082